exposed

exposed

Kimberly Marcus

EMBER

This is a work of fiction. Names, characters, places, and incidents either are the product of the author's imagination or are used fictitiously. Any resemblance to actual persons, living or dead, events, or locales is entirely coincidental.

 Published in the United States by Ember, an imprint of Random House Children's Books, a division of Random House, Inc., New York. Originally published in hardcover in the United States by Random House Children's Books, New York, in 2011.

Ember and the colophon are trademarks of Random House, Inc.

Visit us on the Web! www.randomhouse.com/teens

Educators and librarians, for a variety of teaching tools,
visit us at www.randomhouse.com/teachers

The Library of Congress has cataloged the hardcover edition of this work as follows:
Marcus, Kimberly.
Exposed / by Kimberly Marcus. — 1st ed.
p. cm.
Summary: High school senior Liz, a gifted photographer, can no longer see things clearly after her best friend accuses Liz's older brother of a crime.
ISBN 978-0-375-86693-7 (trade : alk. paper) — ISBN 978-0-375-96693-4 (lib. bdg. : alk. paper) — ISBN 978-0-375-89724-5 (ebook)
[1. Novels in verse. 2. Rape—Fiction. 3. Photography—Fiction. 4. Guilt—Fiction. 5. Best friends—Fiction. 6. Friendship—Fiction. 7. High schools—Fiction. 8. Schools—Fiction.] I. Title.
PZ7.5.M37Ex 2011 [Fic]—dc22 2009051545

ISBN 978-0-375-86591-6 (tr. pbk.)

RL: 4.7

Printed in the United States of America

10 9 8 7 6 5 4 3 2 1

First Ember Edition 2012

Random House Children's Books supports the First Amendment and celebrates the right to read.

This novel is dedicated
in loving memory to my father,

Herb Weiner,

who predicted I would
go into private practice,
write a book,
and appear on *Oprah*.
Well, Dad,
writing is, at its core,
a private practice.
Here's a book.
And, as Meat Loaf sang,
two out of three ain't bad.

exposed

Darkroom Photography, First Period

I am the first one here.

Viewing negatives on the light table,
I find one and itch
to open the chamber
that leads to the darkroom.

Soon, others stroll in:
Javier, the Hoopster.
Nathan, the Nuisance.
Brenda, star of The Brenda Show.

The bell rings as Mrs. Pratt
breezes through the door,
clapping her hands
to get everyone's attention.

Everyone's attention,
I should say,
but mine.

Because nobody needs to tell
Elizabeth Grayson,
Photogirl,
to focus.

Bringing to Light

I slip the photo paper
into the developing solution,
sway it around with black plastic tongs
and wait.

The hum of air from the overhead vent,
the swish of chemicals,
and the sucking in of my breath
are the only sounds shifting
in the dim light of the darkroom.

I'm alone
but not for long.
As white turns to gray,
Kate is with me.
The background of the dance studio blurred
so the focus is all on her—
legs extended in a perfect, soaring split.

The straight line to my squiggle,
my forever-best friend.

In the Hallway, After Last Bell

"Boo!"

The word bursts from my mouth
at the same moment my fingers poke
into each side of her from behind,
and Kate's books drop with a thud.

She whips around in an attempt
to elbow her attacker,
but I'm prepared and jump back
out of her way.

"Liz!" she yelps, then laughs,
waving her hands at my face,
before we reach to re-gather her books
around and between Friday's fleeing feet.

"Just trying to keep you on your toes," I say,
touching her shoulder until it relaxes,
until she gives me a forgiving grin.

"I'm on my toes enough," she says,
and I can't help but smile
at this pointed comeback
from the Mistress of Modern Dance.

"I developed a shot of you dancing today."

Kate shakes her head.
"I can't believe I let you take
pictures of me sweating."

But I tell her my begging paid off,
that this shot is going in my portfolio.

She zips her books
into the safety of her backpack,
scrunches her forehead,
and says I may want to rethink that—
that she would hate for her ugly self
to be the reason I don't get into art school.

I take in her perfect, china-doll complexion,
look straight into her blue-green eyes,
and tell her, "Art schools now require
applicants to submit photos
of the ugliest person they can find.
So you don't have a thing
to worry about."

Friday Night at Salvatore's

We're at our favorite cheesy pizza place:
plastic-coated, red-checkered tablecloths,
Leaning Tower painted on one wall,
a vineyard, maybe Tuscany, on another.

Sal, behind the counter,
white mustache curled in handlebars,
huge belly threatening to burst
through his grease-splattered apron,
singing along to piped-in Italian music.
A walking cliché.

Amanda piles on
Parmesan cheese and hot-pepper flakes.
Dee Dee blots off extra oil with her napkin.
Kate uses a fork and knife
to cut her slice into bite-sized pieces.

By the time my three friends
are finished preparing their meals,
I'm ready for dessert.
"What time should I come by tomorrow?"
Kate asks as we leave.

"I'm staying on the Vineyard
for a few hours after work," I tell her.

"How about seven?"

"Sounds good," she says,
closing the door
on Sal's serenade.

Work

Most of the kids who work
for the Martha's Vineyard Ferry Service,
in the parking lots, at the ticket booth,
or in the concession stands
on the boats, like me,
work during the high season.
A cool summer job.

But keeping my Saturday 8–2 shift
year-round
gives me spending money
and the chance to stay on the island
and hitch a later ferry home to Shoreview.

"See ya, Lizzie-Lou!" my father calls from the bridge
as I make my way down the ramp.

He's just Dad to me,
but to everyone else he's Cap.
Captain Robert Grayson,
King of the Ferry,
Noble Seaman of Nantucket Sound.

Photo Op

I get on my bike
and pedal right out of Vineyard Haven
until I'm winding down country roads
lined with old stone walls and grazing horses.

I lean my bike against an oak
tinted with autumn's promise
and raise my camera to catch a shot
of a wistful woman,
gray hair in a long braid down her back,
patting sweat from her neck
with a green bandana
as she pauses atop her ride-on mower
and stares out across her big yard
at all the grass yet to be mowed.

Saturday Night Slumber

I peel off Kate's Sweet Berry facial mask
and she peels off mine.
We scooch, fresh-faced, onto the couch
and paint each other's nails.

Cotton Candy's what I choose for her
and she, with graceful strokes,
applies a coat of Call Me Crimson
to the tips of my stubby fingers.

When Brian—mmm, Brian—
calls from the diner on his break,
he doesn't ask to see me later.
He knows what night it is:

Saturday Night Slumber.
A Kate and Liz tradition.
Our once-a-month sleepover,
where nothing comes between us.

PMS

We pull photo boxes
onto the den floor
looking for pictures
worthy of a place
in my college portfolio.

We start a YES pile,
a pile for MAYBE,
another for NO.

Kate holds a photo gently at its edges.
"You had really bad PMS that day," she says,
and we both laugh, knowing PMS
has nothing to do with my menstrual cycle
but everything to do with my
"Preparing My Shot" mood,
where everything goes quiet
and I turn in on myself, camera poised,
waiting for the perfect moment
to click.

The Gift

My brother, Mike,
bought me my first camera—
a gift for my twelfth birthday.
He'd seen me eyeing it
in a Hallmark store
at the Cape Cod Mall.

Mike didn't know
I was staring at the camera—
on a shelf beside the scrapbooks
and photo albums—
not because I wanted to take pictures
but because it was lilac,
my favorite color,
and because it had a butterfly on it,
right beside the lens,
made of tiny rhinestones.

He wrapped it himself
with the sports section
of the *Boston Sunday Globe*
and looked down at his feet
when he handed it to me.

The first photo I ever took,
with my very own camera,

I took of Mike that day—
his mouth open wide,
tongue stuck out,
displaying the remains
of his slice of my cake.

Kate's Passion

We're munching on popcorn
as Kate flips channels,
stopping at a documentary
on World War II.

"I think I'll major in history," she says.

"Huh?" I must have heard her wrong.
She's always gotten A's in social studies,
but Kate was born to be a famous dancer
like that Twyla Tharp lady
she gushes about nonstop.

"It's so cool to learn about
what makes the world tick."

The Dance Express has been
Kate's second home since she was four,
and Carol and Steve have rolled out
a bunch of dough from their bakery
to support this love of their only child.

I can't believe, with the way she moves,
that she would want to do anything but dance.
"But you're the Mistress!" I remind her.
"You could be a star!"

"I still love to dance," she says.
"I just don't want to do it professionally."

I think about all her trophies
lining the antique white bureau in her room.
"You're just scared you can't make it, but you can."
It's the same thing we always fight about.

"I don't *want* to make it," she tells me,
shaking her head and taking
her toothbrush from her makeup bag.
"And I won't be able to dance forever."

I follow her into the bathroom off the den.
"You're taking something you love
and putting a time limit on it!"

"Well, some things *are* time-limited," she says,
squeezing toothpaste from the tube,
turning the faucet on.

She looks at my scrunched-up face
in the bathroom mirror,
crosses her eyes to lighten the mood,
and adds, in a booming announcer-type voice,
"But history—everything lives on through history."

Snapshot

We fold out the couch,
tuck in the sheets,
while I search
for a more convincing argument.

Kate's cell phone rings
and she leans over,
fishes for her bag
hidden under crumpled jeans.

"Hey! We're just hangin'.
Yeah, Saturday Night Slumber."
She rolls her eyes, then says,
"Love you, too."

I pretend to yawn,
rest my head on the throw pillow
as if Trevor has put me to sleep.

She comes around the couch
and rips the pillow
out of my hand.

"I'll call you tomorrow," she says to him,
"as soon as I get up."
She rolls her eyes again

and flips the phone shut.

"How's Mr. Whatever-You-Want?" I ask,
having settled on my latest nickname.

"What's that supposed to mean?"

"It means he's whipped," I say.
"He does whatever you want to do."

"That's not true."

Everyone knows and loves Trevor—
solid basketball player,
funny, all-around great guy.

But not everyone knows
that Trevor
is pretty much a doormat
when it comes to Kate.

"Why don't you just break up with him?"

She tells me, "He's a nice guy. And he loves me."

"Yeah, and there are no other
nice guys in the world.
That's it! Stop dancing!
Marry Mr. Whatever!"

I'm half joking, but she glares at me.

"You know what?
I hate when you make up
stupid little names for people.
It's not funny."

She used to think it was funny.

I throw a blanket over the sheets.
"I can't believe you're mad at me,
especially when *you're* the one
who rolls your eyes at everything he says."

"I do not!"
She puts the phone in her bag,
clenches the pillow
with both hands.

"Yes, you do, Kate.
So what do you expect *me* to do?
Say nothing? Be like Trevor?
'Whatever you say goes, sweetie.'
Take a chance for once!"

"Just because he might not be your idea of Prince Charming,
just because I don't want to dance professionally,
just because my plan for my life isn't *your* plan for my life—
that doesn't mean I'm afraid to take a chance."

"Well, I would never let *anything*
get in the way of me taking pictures."

"Yeah," she says.
"That's because you can hide behind your camera."
Her words are like a jab to my gut,
and I want to hurt her.

"That's funny coming from someone
who wants to major in the past
because she's afraid of the future."

She looks like she's about to whip the pillow at me
but then she relaxes her grip and exhales,
tells me I'll never understand.

I've gone too far and I know it,
but she pushed me there.
"Listen—" I say, about to apologize.

She says, "I don't want to hear it,"
puts down the pillow.

I'm mad that she cut me off
and I don't want to say I'm sorry
anymore.

So I tell her I'm going to my room to read.

She gets into bed,
says, "Fine by me,"
leans over
and turns out the light.

Sticks and Stones

I'm in my room
by myself.

I left her downstairs
to mope alone,
to sleep
alone.

Why should I always
apologize first?

I throw my book on the floor,
flip my pillow to the cool side,
and wonder how she can get mad at me
for calling people names.

She always said
she loved the way
I could sum someone up
in a snapshot
or just a few words.

She asked me to come up with a name
for Kevin Foster last year (Boycreep #1)
when I saw him kissing some skank
the day after he dumped her.

She loves it
when I call her the Mistress
and whenever I tell her
she's my forever-best.

Okay, calling her boyfriend
Mr. Whatever
was going a bit too far.
But I call 'em
like I see 'em.

Morning

I look for Kate, but she's gone.
She left, taking my nasty words with her.
I didn't mean to hurt her.
I didn't want her to leave
without giving me a chance
to take the words back.

The Call

There's a lump in my throat
the size of Cape Cod Bay.
I know I've got a big mouth,
but nothing I've said before
ever made her leave.

"I'm sorry, call me,"
I say to the machine.
Then I call Brian.

"I'll pick you up after my shift," he says.
"And make you forget all about Kate."

Oh, Brother

I'm fishing socks out of the dryer an hour later
when Mike comes into the laundry room.

"Hey, Lizzie," he says,
and I catch a whiff of stale beer
as he dumps his clothes
out of his gray duffel bag
into the washing machine.

"When did you come home?" I ask,
handing him the box of detergent.

"Late last night."
He doesn't use the measuring cup,
pours in too much soap.

"After a party?"

"How'd you guess?"

I hold my nose. "Ever hear of toothpaste?"

He cups his hand in front of his mouth
and inhales his own breath.
"Ahh, you don't like Michelob mouthwash?"

I hate to admit—
as he puckers his lips
and pretends to try to kiss me—
that I miss these deep discussions.
So instead I say,
"Hope you don't try to kiss other girls, smelling like that."

Thoughts

When Mike left for college
a month ago
I thought we'd stay close—
maybe even grow closer.

I thought he'd call me up
and invite me down for a visit.
I'd pack a bag
quicker than I could click my camera
and off I'd go
living a college life
if only for a weekend.

I thought when he'd come home to visit
we'd hang out by the docks
and make up boat stories like we used to do—
who's stowing away,
who's sailing off with someone's stolen loot,
who'll wind up on a tropical island
or in a shark's bloated belly.

But I thought wrong.

He hardly ever calls me.
The one trip I took
to Millbrook U

was when I helped lug stuff
into his dorm before Labor Day.

And I only see him now
when a pile of faded jeans
and smelly running gear comes home
crying to be cleaned.

And I don't want to miss him.
But I do.

I Call Again

Carol answers the phone,
tells me Kate came home at dawn,
that she felt sick
and didn't want to wake me.

And I feel sick
knowing she's not.

Bright Penny Beach

"She probably has the flu,
so stop worrying," Brian says
as we pull off our shoes and socks
later that afternoon
and walk along the water's edge.

I love the beach in the fall—
no crowds, no searing heat,
no worrying about how
my bathing suit looks.

I worry less about Kate
when Brian finds
a long, weathered stick
and carves *I love Liz*
into the cold, wet sand
on Bright Penny Beach.

As the tide rushes in
and, with each ebb and flow,
smooths the surface of his words,
I imagine that Neptune himself
is sending our love
on a current from Cape Cod
all the way to Tahiti.

The Travel Channel says
Tahiti
is the most romantic place on earth.

But I stop believing
when Brian
kisses me on the shore
of Bright Penny Beach.

At the Track Last Spring

The first time I noticed him
he was trailing
too close for Mike's comfort
as they ran sprints along the track.

After the whistle, Mike said,
"You better slow down, man,"
smiling, shaking his head
just over the line,
sweat flying off his hair like rain
off a wet dog's coat.

Brian laughed,
patting his glistening neck with a towel,
and told Mike,
"You better speed up."

"You ready to go?" I asked my brother
as I leaned against the chain-link fence,
staring at this shiny new boy.

"Brian, this is my sister, Lizzie.
Lizzie, this is Brian,
just transferred here from Wilton.
He's a junior, like you."

I took in his deep brown eyes,
his sandy blond hair,
his beautiful God-help-me lips
as they formed the word *hello*.

"Check it out, Brian!
My sister's speechless!" Mike teased.

I grabbed Mike's towel from the fence
and whipped it at his head
as Brian smiled.

At me.

Time to Study

"Sorry, I can't stay," Mike says to Mom
as she lays pale blue dinner plates out on the table.

"But we've barely seen you," she says.
"And dinner is ready."

Dad asks, "What's the rush?"

Mike slings his duffel over his shoulder
and grabs a steaming new potato
from the serving bowl,
tossing it from hand to hand to cool it down
before popping it in his mouth.
"I have to study," he says as he chews.

Mom's fingers still cling
to that last piece of stoneware
and I want to tell my brother
he should study
the look on Mom's face,
the way her jaw muscles just went slack
and tightened again in a split second's time.

Left Out to Dry on Sunday Night

No ringing of my cell.
Inbox is empty.
No blink of forgiveness
on the answering machine.

I leave another message,
"Kate, call me. Please call me,"
and my want hangs
heavy on the line.

Best-Friends Collage

I'm putting together a photomontage,
cropped pictures
of Kate and me at our best,
to help put last night behind us.

This 8½-by-11 sheet of paper
isn't big enough
to hold every photo,
so I pick some of my favorites:

Noses, bright red,
our arms draped around
a lopsided snowman
made with six-year-old hands.

Flour on our cheeks,
bowl of batter on the counter,
messy nine-year-olds in too-big aprons
attempting to bake something edible.

Buried up to our necks
in the sand on Bright Penny,
Kate's smile has a gap where a tooth used to be,
must have been seven or eight.

More recent shots, too,
of us being silly,
of us being serious,
of us being us.

I know this collage
is a bit over the top
but I can't help myself.

I've never been good
at guilt.

Making Amends

I see Kate in the hall after first period.
"Hey! Feeling better?" I ask.

She shrugs—"Yeah. A little"—
and tucks a strand of hair behind her left ear.

"I'm sorry about our Slumber," I say,
handing her the collage.

She looks at it, bites her lower lip.
"I'm sorry, too," she says. "I have to go."

"No. Wait!"

But she's already rounding the corner,
disappearing into a sea of students,
and all I can see of her
is her left hand,
fingers clutching the patchwork picture
of friendship.

Whoosh

I just finished developing
the photo of the woman on the Vineyard
and an idea starts swirling.

I leave the darkroom and place my hands
on the edge of Mrs. Pratt's cluttered desk.

"I'm thinking of focusing
part of my portfolio
on Vineyard portraits.
Not of day-trippers or rich summer folks
but off-season shots
of what-you-see-is-what-you-get
year-round islanders."

The swirling turns to a whooshing
as I say the words aloud,
and I hope she likes the idea
because I like the way the whooshing feels.

She leans forward,
clasps her hands around mine
like we're praying together,
and says, "That sounds wonderful."

WHOOSH!

Small Talk

"Hi," I say
at the end of the day
when I catch Kate
coming out of history class.

"Oh! Hi!" she says,
acting surprised to see me,
even though I always meet her here.

We laugh at Mr. Clay's "Staaap running!" squeak
as he reams out some kid down the hall,
and I ask her if we're okay.

She says, "Yes,"
in a distant, formal way
that doesn't sound
okay to me.
"I'm just in a rush."

And as I watch her dash
down the hallway
I wonder if she's rushing to
something important
or rushing away
from me.

Home

Mom's in the kitchen
emptying a bag of groceries
and singing some song about
putting up a parking lot.

I tell her about my portfolio
and she thinks it's a great idea
but worries about me
spending a lot of time
alone on the island.

"Take Brian with you?" she asks,
then immediately shakes her head.
"You wouldn't get much work done that way.
How about Kate?"

I swallow hard. "We had a fight at our Slumber."

"About what?"

"I said mean things about Trevor
and laid into her about not wanting
to major in dance."

Mom puts a loaf of bread on the counter.
"Kate doesn't want to major in dance?"

"See!" I tell her.
"I'm not the only one who thinks that's nuts!"

"Did you apologize?" she asks,
handing me a gallon of milk.

"I tried."

She reaches up
to put a can in the cabinet.
"You and Kate are like sisters.
Everything will work out."

"Yeah," I say. "I hope so."

As I head to my room,
Mom goes back to singing
something about not knowing
what you have until it's gone.

Ridiculous

I grab the catalogs from my desk
and start thumbing through them.
So what if Kate's still mad at me?
I've got better things to think about:
The School of the Museum of Fine Arts,
Parsons,
Rhode Island School of Design.

Packets of possibility.

Fine Dining

Brian's dad brings bundled energy
and a heaping plate of fries
over to the red leather booth I'm sitting in.
"Hi, Liz!" he says.
"Keeping my boy out of trouble?"

"Trying my best."

Brian scoots in next to me,
kisses my cheek,
grabs a fry.

"You've got a half hour left," Mr. Kent says.
"But it's a slow Tuesday
so I'll let you loose."

"Thanks, Dad."

Mr. K high-fives me
before heading back to the kitchen.
Brian points a french fry at my face.
"How ya doin'?"

He shakes the fry a bit before I answer,
"I'm okay."

Yesterday, I gave Kate the collage
and our friendship still doesn't feel
patched up.
But I'm tired of talking about it
so I bite the fry instead.

"How was work?" I ask him as I chew.

"Fine dining at its best," he says,
which he means as a joke.

But you'll find no finer fries
anywhere on Cape Cod.
And no finer boy
than my Diner Boy.

No More Hide-and-Seek

I walk toward the cafeteria
after a bad night's sleep,
which has little to do
with the diner food I ate last night.

Kate, Amanda, and Dee Dee
are up ahead.

Kate sees me, pretends she doesn't,
walks through the double doors.
She's been avoiding me
all week long.

I said I was sorry.
That should be enough.
But it's not and I'm done
playing games.

In the Cafeteria

I sit across from her at our table,
lean forward,
make myself
unavoidable.

Kate focuses on everything but my eyes.
She looks at her hands, the lobe of my left ear.
I take a fumbled cocking-my-head-to-meet-her-gaze step.
She drops her fork and bends down to get it,
perfectly executing the dodge-and-duck dip.

She's the dancer; I'm not graceful,
and this particular routine exhausts me.

"What's wrong with you?" I say.
Amanda and Dee Dee stop eating
and stare at me, at Kate,
at each other.

Kate busies herself
stirring her soup in slow circles,
then says to her spoon, "Nothing's wrong.
I just need some space."

Space?
What does she mean by *that*?

Space from me?

Before I can ask, she stands up,
swings her backpack over her shoulder,
and grabs her tray.

We've always talked out everything
and now she won't tell me anything.

"What the hell is wrong?
I said I was sorry!
It was just a stupid fight!
Besides, isn't Trevor the one you need space from?"

I'm in her face now
and everyone is looking at me
like I'm a lunatic.
And Trevor comes up out of nowhere and says,
"What the hell does *that* mean?"

Kate glares at me like she wants to kill me,
then runs from the room.

I still don't know what her problem is
but I'm trying to convince myself
it's not *my* problem.

I grab my pride and my lunch
and walk away.

And Then There Were Three

"What's up with her?" I ask
when Amanda and Dee Dee
follow me into the bathroom.

I can't believe I'm the one
who doesn't know
what's going on with Kate.
I can't believe *I'm* asking *them*.

We're a foursome
made up of two twosomes,
and although there are three of us in the room,
I'm the one left out.

"She's been quiet with us, too," Dee Dee offers.

Amanda nods and says,
"Maybe she needs some time alone."
She puts her hand on my shoulder.
I swat it away.
What does she know about what Kate needs?

"But why is she avoiding *me*?"
God, I hate how whiny I sound,
but I can't stop.

Amanda says she doesn't know,
and she probably doesn't.
But there's something—
a glint in her eye—
that makes me think Amanda is enjoying
seeing me sweat it out,
enjoying the fact that I have no clue.

"I'll talk to her," she tells me,
hooking her arm into Dee Dee's,
as her constant sidekick
turns to offer me pity
with big doe eyes.

Advanced Portfolio

Mrs. Pratt makes her way
from table to table,
looking at each of our portfolios.

She's looking at my stuff now,
bent over, all serious,
and my stomach
is fighting its way up my throat.

She spoke to every other kid
but she says nothing to me,
just grabs one of my pictures
and holds it up over her head.

"This, my friends, is a perfect shot."

As she puts the picture back on the table
she leans to me and whispers,
"Liz, you can go places."

Perfect Shot

The young boy's face is bursting with energy:
openmouthed grin,
eyebrows arched,
gray-green eyes wide with wonder—
sparkling even—
as he cranes his neck
around the larger boy in front of him in line,
to get a good view
of the Flying Horses Carousel.

When I zoomed in on him last summer
the other tourists, flashing lights,
piped-in organ music
faded away—
PMS to the max.

He'd been tapping his head—
tap, tap, tap—
with both hands, knobby elbows flared.
I caught the shot in between taps,
just as his hands left his head.

Hands too far from his skull—
questioning.
Hands too close—
confusion.

But midway,
midway it worked.
It did what I wanted it to do.

It captured emotion.
Pure exhilaration.

Like a Bird

I'm floating up
flying high
swirling around
soaring
out of my mind
with glee.
Until it hits me,
midair,
that the person
I most want to tell
has flown away.

Second Most

I head to the gym at the end of the day
to catch Brian before track practice.
He comes out of the locker room
and I run to him
to tell him what Mrs. Pratt said.

"That's great, babe!" he says,
and gives me a hug.

I pull the picture out.
"This one?" he asks,
taking it from me.
"It's nice."

My stomach muscles clench.
"Nice?"

"No! I mean, it's really good!" he says,
trying to recover.
"I'm proud of you."

The coach blows his whistle,
and the guys head over to the bleachers.

"I gotta go, babe. I'll see ya later. Okay?"

"Yeah. Sure," I say
as he squeezes my hand
then sprints away.
"That would be *nice*."

Third Time's the Charm

When I get home
I tell Mom what Mrs. Pratt said
and she calls Dad at work,
has to shout
over the blare of the ferry horn.

Dad shouts back,
"WAHOO! That's my girl!"
says "That's my girl!" again,
louder, even though
the horn has stopped blowing.

Family Pride

Dad's always been proud of me.
Whether I was playing a potato
in the Fabulous Food Groups play,
or skimming my Sunfish sailboat along the shore,
or winning a hot-dog-eating contest
in junior high.

Mom's proud of me, too.
Though I know she wished I were the apple,
wished I spent less time on the water
and more time on my homework,
wished the prize was not a month's supply
of artery-clogging wieners.

Start Your Engines

In the morning, before school,
I see Kate in the parking lot.

She raises her eyebrows,
opens her mouth
like she wants to call out to me.

But then a car backfires
and she spins on her heels and zooms away,
widening the distance between us.

Phone a Friend

Amanda calls on Friday night.

"Kate seems okay to me she said she's just had a lot going on lately with school and dance and I asked her why she's mad at you and she says she's not so stop worrying."

I snort into the receiver and roll my eyes
as she pauses for a much-needed breath.
"Thanks, Amanda. That explains everything."

"No problem! Glad to help!"

Amanda's dad is a psychologist
and she wants to go to college
and follow in his footsteps.
God help us all.

Toppings

I get off the boat in Vineyard Haven
after six hours of stocking napkins,
wiping counters,
ladling clam chowder into
Styrofoam cups.

I walk past the Welcome Center,
not empty, because it's a mild Saturday,
but not teeming with day-trippers
waiting for buses or cabs
or a ticket back home.

I head up the street
half a block
and cross over to the other side
so I can get a wide shot
of a girl in ripped jeans,
tattoos and piercings, sitting,
knees up, head back, eyes closed
in front of Crazy Cows Ice Cream Shop—
weathered shingles, windows shut,
padlocked door—
sign next to her reads
FLAVORS OF THE WEEK.

Distraction

Calvin James,
pitcher for the Shoreview Sharks,
throws great parties,
and Kate's at a dance competition in Boston
so there's no danger of seeing her here,
no danger of me
crowding her sacred space.

She's not returning my calls.
She's making plans without me.
She's pretending she doesn't see me
when I pass her in the hall.
I've been too consumed with her.

So I go
to be okay without her.
To be with Brian
and be okay
without her.

And except for a few times
every few minutes,
I hardly think about Kate
at all.

In Calvin's Kitchen

"Now I know, now I know," Amanda sings,
giddy from beer
and wearing a stupid grin.
"I know why Kate won't talk to you."

This knowledge is fun for her,
but my icy stare lets her know
I'm in no mood for games.
She hops up on the counter
and bumps her heels
against the wood-grained cabinet.

"Callie told Dee Dee that Mike told Tanner that he and Kate were doing the wild thing at your house last weekend while you were asleep."

Now I know.

Once Upon a Time

When we were six
Kate told me
that when we grew up
she would marry Mike
so we could be sisters and best friends
at the same time.

When we were twelve
I found his class picture
in her desk drawer—
a heart drawn on the back
in pink pen.

When we were fourteen
Kate's body started changing
and she'd laugh when Mike said,
"Looking good, Katie."

Did he say that this time?

This time,
did she do more
than laugh?

Some Nerve

"I can't believe you," I say,
standing at Kate's door Sunday morning.
She looks at me,
confused.

"When I said you should dump Trevor,
it wasn't an invitation to mess around with *Mike*."

Her eyes grow wide.
Her face pales.

"I'm not thrilled, Kate,
but it's nothing to freak out about.
It's no reason to treat *me*
like *I* did something wrong."

She moves, barefoot,
onto the cold front steps
and closes the door behind her.
"Who said I messed around with Mike?"

"Mike told Tanner and—"

"Mike told Tanner?"
Her eyes bug out of her head.

"He said something about a wild night."

Kate bites hard on her lower lip,
so hard it turns white.
I can tell her mind's racing,
but she doesn't say a thing.

"Well, did you?" I ask.

She looks like a rabbit frozen in light.
"We didn't have sex."

"Fine, but something happened.
Did you guys kiss?"

She closes her eyes and I know it's true.
"I'm sorry, Liz. I can't . . . ," she says.

I'm mad
she fooled around with my brother.
I'm mad
she's been treating me like crap.

But I push the anger inside
because big, fat tears
are rolling down her cheeks
and I can count on one hand
the times I've seen her cry.

"It's okay, Kate.
No big deal."
I reach out to touch her arm.
"I'll tell everyone
Mike's delusional."

If I wasn't so relieved
to finally know what's wrong,
I might be offended
as she pushes my hand away,
tells me she has to go,
and heads back inside.

"You're an Ass"

You have reached Mike and Jordan.
We're too busy studying
to pick up the phone.
Please leave a message at the beep.

Homeroom, Monday Morning

"Did you talk to Kate?
Is Mike the reason she broke up with Trevor?"
Amanda's wearing that dumb old smirk
and shifting her eyebrows up and down.

"She broke up with Trevor?"

"Yesterday," Amanda said.
"He said he'd forgive her and she broke up with him anyway.
I hope the night was worth it."

"Get a life," I say.
"Mike has an active imagination."

She opens her notebook
but won't let it go.
"I hear Kate's pretty active herself," she says,
and I know she's joking but I'm not in the mood.

I lean across the aisle
and her notebook falls to the floor,
revealing a long list of guys' names
written on the back
(some with one heart, some with two,
some scratched out completely).

"Leave Kate alone," I say.
"She doesn't want to talk about it."

Amanda bends over, grabs the notebook,
and mumbles loud enough for me to hear,
"Maybe she just doesn't want to talk about it with *you*."

Big Men in a Small Town

This wouldn't be such big news
if Kate hadn't cheated on
the dream date of so many
gossipy girls.

Trevor's got his fan club here,
and if they trash-talk Kate,
maybe he'll notice them.

This wouldn't be such big news
if Mike weren't so fast on his feet,
but his trophies and photographs
and clippings from the *Cape Cod Times*
line a display case in a hallway
of Shoreview High.

He's got his props here,
making it all look so easy.

Trouble is, now his big head
and his big mouth
make Kate
look easy, too.

Fanning the Flame

I am the firefighter,
putting out tiny rumors
before they have time to grow and spread.

"Kate did not sleep with Mike!"
"She doesn't own a lacy bra!"
"My parents didn't barge in on them!"
"She is *not* a two-timing slut!"

But whenever Kate sees me
she proceeds to the nearest exit
like I'm the fire.

Trippin'

Mrs. Pratt clucks her tongue and tells us
that on Sunday, November 16,
the School of the Museum of Fine Arts
is hosting National Portfolio Day
at the Hynes Convention Center in Boston.

This is a huge event where college recruiters
will look at our portfolios
and give us tips to make our photos pop.

I've had the day circled
on my calendar for months.
Still, my heart skips a beat
as she says the date out loud.

"I've arranged for transportation
for those who plan to go," she says.
"It's a great opportunity to see
what schools are looking for."

The bell rings like a starter gun
and an image plays out in my head:
college recruiters hurdling over tables,
knocking kids to the floor,
to grab what they're looking for—
my portfolio.

Footwork

I stepped up to the plate on Monday,
stepped on the rumors since then,
careful to step around
my friend's bruised ego.

Now it's Thursday
and I thought things would be better,
but Kate's still avoiding me,
and walking on eggshells isn't easy to do.

My shell cracks when she pretends
she doesn't see me as she heads down the stairs.

Letting Her Have It

"Get over it, Kate!
Let it go already!"

We're at the bottom of the stairwell,
near the emergency exit,
my body now positioned to keep hers
from flying back up the stairs.

"Everyone will stop talking about it
if you stop letting them think
it was such a big deal."

Letting Me Have It

She's silent
for a long minute.
Then she looks straight at me,
straight through me,
and tells me
why
it was such a big deal.

Mike

My brother is a track star.
My brother is a partier.
My brother is a bit of a chauvinist pig.
My brother, even when he annoys me,
is someone I love.

My brother is not
who Kate says he is.

My brother
is not
a rapist.

"Mike Raped Me"

Her words bring white-hot pain,
like my gut is being sliced open by a doctor
who forgot to give me drugs.

I want to scream at her
because she must be lying,
but my voice is small and far away
and all I can manage is,
"What are you *saying*?!?"

And she is small and far away
and she says,
"I can't."

And she tries to move past me,
but I need more.
I deserve more.
I won't let her go.
"Talk to me!"

She looks to the staircase
then over her shoulder toward
the emergency exit.
She runs for it,
my "*Please!*" drowned out
by the shrill of the door's alarm.

Under the Stairs

Under the stairs that lead
from the upper level of my house to the landing
and down again to the den in the basement,
there's a closet.

Behind a rack of musty-smelling coats,
out of size, out of style, or both,
and suits that Dad hasn't worn in years,
that closet curves around to a sloping crawl space
too small for storage, but just the right size
for a little girl.

When that little girl was me
I would bring my dolls or my crayons or,
when she wasn't looking,
Mom's Divine Rouge lipstick
to that secret space.

I'd pull the string, with the knot on the end,
that hung from the bare bulb,
and push past the garments
that separated my real life
from my imagination.

More than anything, I wish
I could fit into that closet now.

A Not-So-Simple Question

"How are things?" Mom asks
when I come in the door.

What do I do? WhatdoIdo??

I want to tell her but I'm freaking out
and having her freak out now, too,
would only make things worse.

Luckily, I don't have to tell her
because she's not waiting for an answer.
"Mike left a message for you," she says.
"Said to tell you he was calling you back."

I'll figure out how to tell Mom and Dad later.

Right now,
I have something to tell my brother.

He Says

"I would never hurt Kate!
We had sex! I didn't
rape her!"

He says she was sleeping on the couch
and woke up when he brought his bag
down to the laundry room.

He says they talked
and then he kissed her.
He says she kissed him back.
"Then we had sex. It was just sex, Lizzie."

"That's not what *she* says."

He asks me why he'd even tell his friends
he had sex with Kate if he raped her—
why he would be that stupid.

And I guess he has a point
because my brother could not be
that stupid.

Signs

She had no bruises
that I could see.
No cuts, no swollen eyes.

I saw no scratches,
next morning, on Mike.
So which one's telling lies?

Keeping Secrets

I can't believe this is happening.
I'm about to hang up the phone
but Mike says something that stops me.
"It's not like it was the first time we hooked up."

"What?"

He keeps talking.
"We never had sex before.
But we kissed. Last year."

I can feel the hairs tingle
on the back of my neck.
"When?"

I scan my brain for any memory
of Kate telling me anything
close to this.
I get nothing.

"One night in the kitchen,
while you were sleeping downstairs.
She came up to get something to drink
and I was having a late-night snack."
Mike forgets that Cap'n Crunch
is supposed to be a breakfast food.

"Foster just dumped her
and she started crying,
then we kissed for a while."

"How come you didn't tell me?"

"She didn't want you to know.
Figured you'd be mad or something.
Said you always said I was 'off-limits.'"

Now I know my brother's
telling me the truth
because I used those exact words
many times,
joking but not really.

Off-Limits

We sat on the front steps,
the sun hanging low,
and watched him
come up the driveway after a run
taking deep breaths, hands on his hips.

She said he was her prince
in sweaty sneakers.
I laughed and said
he was off-limits.

We chased his car, waving,
as he left to take Mary Draper
to the junior prom.
She said, "He looks cute in that tux."

"Put your eyes back in your head," I said.
"He's off-limits."

When we watched him
play football
in the backyard with his friends
she said, "He could tackle me anytime."

"No, he can't," I said.
"He's off-limits."

She didn't listen,
kept secrets from me,
cheated on Trevor,
crossed the line
with *my* brother.

Five Minutes Later

Mike calls back,
tells me I've got to set her straight,
that it was just sex.

Tells me not to tell Mom and Dad.
"They'll kill me if they knew
I had sex in the house."

There's a pleading in his voice
that stirs something inside me.

Before I can say anything, he says,
"Who else has she told?"

Panic

Panic makes its way up my spine
like ice water through a straw—
who else has she told?

Who Can I Tell?

Brian makes it over here
in ten minutes flat.
I swear to myself I won't cry
but before his dented chariot
pulls out of the driveway
his shoulder is drenched.

He puts his foot on the brake
but I flap my hands,
telling him to keep going.

He heads toward Bright Penny,
but I don't want to pollute our beach.
So I make him pull into the deserted parking lot
behind the town hall,
and we sit on a worn wooden bench
where everything spills out of me:
thick, sticky, black,
like oil.

A Mess the Morning After

It's always pitch-black
in the room off the darkroom
where we process film into negatives.
If the tiniest bit of light gets in
it can ruin the roll.

It took me a long time to get used to
loading the film onto the development reels
in the dark
but I've gotten so good at it
that everyone asks for my help.

I'm helping Carla right now,
Carla with zero personality,
large, yellowed teeth,
and a good photographic eye.

But I can't get my fingers to work
at all
and I'm pretty sure I've destroyed
all the shots she took
at her family-with-big-teeth reunion
and I'm spilling solution
all over the place.

But I'm glad for the darkness.

Otherwise, Zero P
would see
I'm spilling tears, too.

Watching

When I come out of science class
I see Kate by her locker,
smiling while Amanda gabs away.

I can't hear Amanda's words,
but how can Kate be smiling?

At the Sink

I come out of the stall in the girls' room
to find Kate
staring in the mirror.
Panic spreads
across her face when she sees me.

"Will you talk to me?" I ask.

She's shaking her head and I know
she's about to say no
and I don't want her to say no
so I tell her that Mike said
he would never hurt her.

Her eyes don't move.
They're fixed on me.
"You believe Mike."

She hits the button on the soap dispenser
again and again,
but there's nothing left.

I ask her what I'm supposed to think when
she won't tell me anything.

"I told you he raped me," she says.

"What else do you need to know?"

"I need to know why
you kissed him last year
and never told me."

There's a crazy-scary fire in her eyes.
"I'm not surprised he told you that.
He wants you to take his side.
I bet he didn't tell you about the pillow."

I ask her what she's talking about
and she says, "Figures."

She shuts down.
I can actually see her shutting down,
body sagging, eyes closing,
head tilted to the side.
I'm losing her.

There are things I should say
but I can't speak.

She turns away
and the nagging question,
the one I shouldn't ask but I need to ask,
pushes out of my mouth.
"Kate, have you told anyone else?"

"No," she says, and I close my eyes,
waiting for the words *not yet*,
but the *wrrshhhhh* of the hand dryer
and the solid closing of the door as she leaves
are the only sounds bouncing
off the tiled walls.

Red Eyes

There's a light tap-tap on my shoulder
as I grab my coat from my locker.
I spin around, hoping it's Kate,
but Trevor's standing there—
one hand scratching the back of his head,
the other shoved
deep in the pocket of his jeans.

"Hi, Trevor."

He doesn't say hi back,
just blurts out,
"Is Kate okay?"

I'm not sure how to answer this.
I'm not sure what he knows.
I look straight into his eyes
and see that they're rimmed with red.

I look at this crumpled boy
and wonder if Kate
would have kissed Mike,
would be accusing him of rape,
if I hadn't picked on Trevor,
hadn't told her to take a chance.

He stares at a spot on the floor.
"She broke up with me."

I tell him I know,
and he walks away
looking like a lost dog,
leaving me filled
with so much sorry.

Slumber-Party Games

When I get home I call Mike.
He picks up on the first ring.
He says he knows nothing about a pillow
except that maybe
they were tossing one around
on the couch,
and he can't understand why
she's saying these things.

I hear that pleading again,
the tone a younger Mike used
when Mr. Rubin, Little League coach,
failed to believe Mike didn't steal
Scott Rubin's glove,
identical to the glove Mike wore.
Scott, who couldn't run bases to save his life.

Failed to believe him
until Scott
found his glove
beneath the bleachers.

Straight To . . .

It's late Friday afternoon
and the sky is turning
the color of pumpkins.

Dad asks,
as we rake leaves into piles,
how things are going.

"They're going," I say,
and I pray he doesn't need
more than that.

I pray he doesn't ask me
where they're headed.

Happy Girl

I'm happy to be on this ferry today.

Happy to be away from school,
away from my parents,
who should probably know
what I can't tell them.

Happy to be training Randall,
who can't even manage
to work a microwave,
who doesn't know me at all.

It's cold on this early afternoon.
Gray clouds hover, not allowing me
to shoot film in the best possible light.

But I am happy.
Happy, that's me.

High-Speed Film

I take a zillion pictures:
weathered rowboats lined up
on the strip of shore along Beach Road,
scrub pine, driftwood,
rusty blue bike, long abandoned.

I used to take photos a few times a week,
but now my camera fills my afternoons,
my weekends, the holes in my life
that Brian can't fill.

I used to take time to look,
to see.

But now time is something to get through,
so I aim and shoot at everything
crossing my line of vision.

Party Boy

Mike shows up at Kyle Jagbee's party.
He's not supposed to be here.
He's supposed to be at school,
but he used to run track with Kyle
and Mike's always up for a party.

I'm hanging in the den,
my camera focused on Brian
celebrating his team's big win,
when something crashes out on the patio.

Along with everyone else,
I run out back
and find Mike lying on the ground,
while his best friend, Tanner,
slams his fist into Mike's face.

Damage Control

"What did you do?"
I hiss in his ear,
helping him into the patio chair,
blood dripping from his nose.

"I was just joking around with Callie
and Tanner went nuts," he says,
as if there's nothing wrong with
hitting on his best friend's girlfriend.

"Like you joked around with Kate?" I ask,
watching drops of blood pool on his sneaker.

I'm sure I look like the caring sister
as I grab a napkin lying near
the shattered glass of the overturned table
and hand it to him.

"I told you," he whispers,
his voice full of gravel,
"I didn't rape her."

I believe him.
But I'm pissed that he ruined the party,
pissed that he fooled around with my forever-best,
so I tell him to try telling that to Kate.

He reaches out
for his half-empty bottle of beer
but I grab the bottle before he can
and throw the beer in his face.

Then I leave him
brewing.

A Caring Sister

A caring sister
might worry
when rubber burns in the driveway
and Mike's car peels off.

But all
I feel
is relief.

Stunned

It's three a.m. and two policemen
are at the door.

I thought Mike
drove back to school,
but when the doorbell rang
he emerged from the den,
all bloodshot eyes and Mentholyptus breath.

Mom and Dad stand there
as a cop asks Mike where he was
earlier tonight.

Mike tells the cops he was at a party.

Dad rubs his hands across his face
and Mom looks hard at my brother
when he admits that, yes, he did leave the party
and go to the home of Katherine Morgan
at approximately twelve-thirty a.m.

Dad crosses his arms
and Mom's mouth falls open
when he admits to throwing rocks at her window
and taking off when Kate's dad
came barreling out of the house.

Dad tells Mike not to say anything else, asks the cop,
"Are you charging my son with something here?"

Mom moves toward my brother,
like she's the track star,
when the old cop with the pockmarked face
says they have a warrant for Mike's arrest.

"He's being arrested
for throwing pebbles at a window?" Dad yells
as Mom grabs Mike by the arm,
a vein threatening to explode
in her long, thin neck.

The older cop looks at Dad and says,
"No, sir. Your son is being charged with rape."

Mike's face loses color, our eyes meet,
and he looks and sounds like he's about to cry.
"I told you, Lizzie. I *swear* I didn't do it!"

"There must be some mistake!" Dad says
when the younger cop asks my brother
to place his hands behind his back,
asks my mother to take her hand off Mike's arm
as he reaches to his belt for the cuffs.

"Don't worry! We're right behind you!" Mom calls out
when the cops lead my brother to the squad car.

My parents stand there
a second longer.
Then they turn
to me.

What I Know

"What do *you* know about this?" Mom asks,
yanking off her robe.

I shiver, sure as if I'm lying naked in snow.

I tell her that Kate says rape
and Mike says not.
That it happened at our Slumber
after I went upstairs.

She grabs for her coat.
"After the big fight?"

"It wasn't a big fight!" I yell
as guilt spreads its wings like a falcon,
talons clawing my gut,
digging in.

The Best Trick

When we were small
Mike and I thought
Dad's friend from college
was better than Houdini,
the way he could make coins
vanish into thin air.

But now Uncle Nate's traded his pouch of change
for a law degree and a Brooks Brothers suit,
and it's my dad who's on his cell phone
heading out the door, hoping Uncle Nate can make this
nightmare disappear.

Priorities

I should be sound asleep,
dreaming of Brian
sailing me away to Tahiti.

Instead, I'm staring at the ceiling
imagining my parents at the police station—
warped scenes from *Law & Order*
playing out in my head—
worrying about my brother,
hating Kate for pressing charges,
and missing my forever-best friend.

Almost Morning

They speak in hushed tones.
They think I'm sleeping.
"What are we going to do?" she asks.
"I don't know," he says.

Bedsprings creak, and I picture my mother
propping her back up against the headboard.
"Why would she say such things?"
"Shhh," says Dad, "lower your voice."

But my mother,
the lady with a kind word for everyone,
Kate's second-biggest fan,
doesn't lower her voice one bit
when she calls Kate a bitch.

Bad Dream, Bad Girl

I'm screaming at Mike.
Why did you go there?
Why did you go there?

He squints at me
as if I'm asking
the dumbest question on earth,
and tells me he went there
because I told him to.

My eyes shoot open
and I remember the last words
I spoke to him before he took off:
Try telling that to Kate.

Unspoken Concern

What was it like
to spend the night in jail?
Was it dirty?
Did you sleep?
Were you scared?

I can't bring myself
to ask these questions
as he comes through the door.

But I wonder.

Wants

Brian hurries to wipe grease from his hands
as soon as he sees me walk
into the diner.

I don't know what I look like
but my look
has him concerned enough
to tell his dad he needs to take his break
now
at the height of Sunday brunch.

He tries to usher me
into a booth
but I shake my head and walk outside.
He follows.

"Mike spent the night in jail.
Kate pressed charges."

"Holy shit!"
His hands fly up to hold the sides of his head
and I can see dried ketchup stuck to his elbow.

"I can't believe this," I say.

"Neither can I," he says,
looking at his dad peering out
the glass door of the diner, tapping his watch.
"I don't think I can get off right now."

"It's okay," I say,
wanting to be by myself—
wanting him
to not let me be alone.

Something to Cling To

Nothing is steady
except for the feeling
of my camera in my hand.

Then and Now

I spent the first semester last year
trying to figure out
how to adjust the camera settings
to get the right exposure,
how to make a test strip,
a contact sheet,
how to develop and enlarge a print.
I never thought it would make sense
and debated dropping out of class.

But now my fingers move
over the controls
and my brain knows—
because of the amount of light,
the film speed, the type of picture I want to take—
exactly what I need to do.

Working with
my manual camera
has become
automatic.

No Escape

Every spot I find to take photos
is a memory.

The park
across from Shoreview Heights Beach
where Mike played ball—
me and Kate watching the games
from nearby swings.

The beach
where Kate and I sunned and swam.
She, a graceful dolphin.
Me, splashing around like someone
in need of a lifeguard.

I force myself to focus on the smaller picture—
the diamond pattern
in the rusting chain-link backstop
behind home plate—
the stones of the jetty,
snails clinging,
to avoid being sucked out to sea.

Ouch

I'm laying on my bed, lights out,
facing the wall
when Mom comes in and sits beside me.
I feel her warm hand on my back.

"Sweetie, I know this is hard for you.
I don't like the idea of Mike having sex with Kate
but that's what happened.
Mike would never force her.
Guilt can do ugly things to people
and it's done ugly things to Kate."
My back stiffens, but I don't turn to face her.
"I don't think you should talk to Kate anymore,
but if you do"—
and she says it like I should—
"tell her that it's not too late to take it all back.
It's not too late to make it go away."
She kisses the back of my head before she leaves.

My mother has pinned
all her hopes on me.
And I can't pull out
the pins.

Monday Morning

Instead of being back at Millbrook
in faded jeans and sneakers,
Mike's got on his navy blazer.

Dad's wearing a dark gray suit
and Mom's in lavender linen,
their faces tightly pressed,
as they head to the courthouse
where my brother will be charged.

I watch them go
from my bedroom window,
in my wrinkled cotton pj's,
skipping school because I feel like crap.

Physical or psychological?
Who gives a shit.

I'm staying right here.

Knowing

Brian calls at noon and tells me
it's a good thing I stayed home.
"They're talking about it, babe."

I hang up the phone and cry,
because knowing they would
doesn't make
knowing they are
any easier.

Gotcha

I imagine
being downstairs that night
in my secret space,
door ajar just enough
for me to lean out
slightly to the left
and catch a glimpse
of what's happening
on the pullout couch
camera raised
shot taken
indisputable handheld truth.

Feet

I'm back in bed an hour later
looking at a photo
of the soles of Kate's feet.
I took it last spring
for an assignment:
Take a picture that represents Work.

Kate agreed
only after I promised
not to tell anyone the feet belonged
to her.

There's work in these feet.
Old work: a rough callus
on the ball of her left foot.
New work: a blister,
shiny and exposed
on the tip of her right pinky toe.

Soft blur of the background
highlighting the hard work
of strong, solid feet.

If I can convince Kate
to let me take pictures of her sweating,
to let me take pictures of her feet,

I can convince Kate
to do
anything.

Monday Afternoon at the Dance Express

I'm in the parking lot
imagining her
trying to lose herself
in the sway of the music,
in the movement of her limbs.

I wait a bit for the dancers to clear.
Some say, "Hi, Liz,"
thinking, I'm sure,
that I'm here, as usual,
to meet up with my best friend.

And each simple greeting
is like the scraping of a fingernail
against a fresh scab.

Convincing Kate

When Kate comes out
I beg her to talk to me,
beg her to drop the charges.
She shakes her head, tells me she can't,
kicks a pebble with her sneaker.

When I ask her if she can't or she won't
she leans against the brick wall of the building,
bites her lower lip, and tells me I should go.

When I scream, "Mike says it was just sex!"
she throws her black nylon dance bag
onto the ground
and gets right up in my face.

"Just sex?" she says.
"Just *sex*?"

Those two words and
the dam
breaks.

She Says

She says she was sleeping on the couch
and woke up when he came in
and they talked for a while
and then he kissed her
and she didn't mind
even though he had beer on his breath.

She says he said,
"Hey, you're beautiful."

She says he got on top of her
and she told him to get off
but he wouldn't move
so she told him she'd yell
if he didn't get off of her
now
and she was sure he would
but he didn't and she says it again,
"But he didn't."

She says that instead he said,
"Shhh, Katie. You're so beautiful."

She says he took the throw pillow
with the pink and yellow flowers
from under her head and put it over her face.

She says he said,
"We're just having fun."

She says the pillow smelled musty and it was hard to breathe and one arm was pressed between her body and the couch and she hit him and tried to scratch him on the back with her other hand but he grabbed it and pushed it under her body and she thought her shoulder would pop and he rubbed his hands all over her.

She says he said,
"Nice, Katie."

She says she tried to scream again and he pressed the pillow harder and grabbed at her sweatpants and her underwear and got them down below her knees and he felt so heavy and she couldn't breathe, couldn't breathe and then it hurt ithurtsobad and then he was done.

And she's looking at me
but she's not here anymore.
And I open my mouth
to say something to bring her back
but she holds her palm out
as if she might wave good-bye,
and says he moved the pillow.

He moved the pillow and she could breathe and she was so happy she could breathe

and he ran his fingers through her hair and she jumped up,
pulled her pants back on.

She says he said,
as she ran for the stairs,
"Hey, you're something."

$a \neq b$

It's mild out but I'm freezing.
There's a pressure in my head
that doesn't feel right.
And "It was just sex, Lizzie"
does not add up
to this.

I'm Sorry

I reach out for her
but she holds her arms
tight around her middle,
tears streaming,
and, for the first time ever,
she apologizes before I do.

"I'm sorry, Liz,
but I can't be with you anymore.
Every time I'm with you,
I see him."

I know I should say something soothing,
but I didn't expect this.
I did not expect her
to be done
with me.

She's crying hard now.
So am I.
"This isn't my fault!" I say.
She says she knows.

"I thought we were friends!
Forever-best friends!"

"We were," she whispers,
and I have to strain to hear,
watching her breath form a white cloud
as it hits the autumn air
and disappears.

Empty

I run,
not knowing where I'm going, but I run.
Around the building, down the street,
my sneakers smacking the pavement so hard,
shooting fire up my shins.

I run past twelve years of friendship,
matching clothes and birthday parties,
jumping on beds and catching crickets,
too-long phone calls and belly laughs,
passing notes and building dreams.

Mold

When I get home I run downstairs,
grab the pillow from the couch,
hold it close to my nose
and gag.

Flesh and Blood

Could someone I've lived with,
someone I love and trust,
do something so heinous?

Am I related to
this?
To someone capable of
this?

This and That

My eyes move back and forth
scanning the shelf in my room
until I find what I'm looking for.

I pull down an album of family photos
and flip through, faster and faster,
until all the memories
blur together
like those tiny books
he and I used to love,
with stick figures that seem to move
in one fluid motion
when you fan the pages quickly
with your thumb.

I stop at a snapshot,
Halloween.
I think I was six.

This boy, wrapped head to toe in gauze,
the only one able to lure a princess
in a pink gown, jeweled tiara,
and scuffed white sneakers
out of her castle by convincing her
that Frankenstein,
coming down the front walk

of the Cohens' house,
was just a kid wearing a mask
to hide a monster zit.

This boy, who held her hand
that whole evening long,
even when his friends ran past
spraying shaving cream
and calling to him to ditch Cinderella.

This boy, who helped her conquer her fear
and collect her treats.

How can *this* boy be *that* guy?

Because of Him

Because of Mike,
I found Brian.
Because of Mike,
I lost Kate.

Monday Night Dinner

Mom spoons rice onto her plate,
passing the bowl to Dad,
as Mike
shoves food into his mouth like it's his last meal.

"What happened in court?" I ask.
Mom's back stiffens, then relaxes.
She asks if we can just have a normal dinner.
Normal?

Dad sets the rice bowl on the table
and tells me that Mike was charged,
a court date set.
Mom slams her fork down and glares at Dad.
"When is it?" I ask.

Mom says, "In about six months,"
and pleads, "Can we eat now?"
But she doesn't eat.
She pushes her rice around a bit,
shakes her head,
and leaves the room.

Dad takes his napkin from his lap,
wipes each corner of his mouth,
and goes after her

as Mike and I stare at each other
from opposite sides of the table.

"I didn't do it, Lizzie.
Do you really think I could do that?"

"Kate told me everything," I say
as I bring my full plate to the sink.

Everything

"*I* told you everything!"

"Not the same everything!"

He slams his fists on the table.
"That's because she's lying!"

"So you didn't hold a pillow over her face?"
That freezes him.

"Is that what she said?" His voice cracks.
"What else did she say?"

I say nothing.

He stands up fast, his chair falling to the floor.
"Lizzie! Holy shit! I would never do that!"

My father appears in the doorway.
"Your mom's not feeling well! Quiet down!"

Mike turns to him.
"Dad, Kate told Liz a bunch of lies about that night."

"Lizzie?" Dad moves toward me.
"What did she say?"

"Nothing! She said nothing!"

I push past him and run to my room
trying to remember something—
trying to remember if Kate said *no*.

Thinking When Drinking

Maybe he thought
if she didn't say no
that meant she was saying
yes.

I know she didn't want it
but maybe he thought she did.

Back to School

In the corner of the main lobby
before Tuesday's first bell,
Amanda, Dee Dee,
and other girls drawn to drama
crowd around Kate, hugging her,
whispering in her ear.

Her body is tight and I know
the last thing she wants is a pity party.

I want to rush over,
take her hand, pull her away.
But I didn't make the guest list.

News Is Spreading

Determined to prove I can handle this
I walk to class chin up,
even though Kate won't talk to me,
even though I look like the bad guy—
same high-set cheekbones,
same cleft in our chins.

I'll Never Be Able to Make Up for This

I'll join Habitat for Humanity.
I'll bring food to the hungry.
I'll teach the illiterate to read.
I'll walk for miles, barefoot,
to raise money for sick children.
I'll volunteer every weekend
at the Seaside Home for the Elderly.
I'll even donate every drop of my blood.

But will the hospital
take blood
from me?

Wednesday's Child

Dee Dee finds me
in the art room,
chin down,
avoiding the cafeteria.
"Are you okay?" she asks.

I am so grateful for concern
that it takes all my effort not to cry.
All I can manage is a shrug.

She tells me everything will work out and
I know that's the biggest of fattest lies,
but I grab on to it anyway.
"I hope you're right," I say.

She squeezes my arm and leaves.
She doesn't ask me to join her
in the cafeteria.
She doesn't offer to eat her lunch
here with me.
She doesn't tell me that she's on her way
to have lunch with Kate,
even though
I know she is.

Passing Notes

Amanda passes me a note in homeroom
and I open it,
happy that she's trying to make a connection.

Kate dropped out of dancing
and her mom's taking her
to a therapist next week.
Just thought you'd want to know.

I'm glad Kate's going to therapy
but the fact that she quit dancing altogether
makes me want to cry.

And the fact that Amanda sits there
all smug with her insider info
makes me want to shove
this note down her throat.

But I take the paper
and those feelings,
fold them up tight,
and tuck them away.

Holding It Together

"I'm fine, thanks," I say
every time Mrs. Pratt asks how I'm doing,
a smile pasted on my face
with Please-God-Save-Me Glue.

Gossip

I'm at the library after school
cramming for a physics test.

I look up and see
Jen Millson and Sari Cobb,
two girls I hardly know,
in the stacks near my table.

They're talking about Mike.

They say he had a knife
and that he told Kate
he would slice her up
if she tried to scream.

I walk over to them,
but before I can say
"He did *not* have a knife!"
they grab their books and check out.

My Muse

When I get to Mrs. Pratt's room today
there's a quote
written in bright blue marker
on the assignment board beside her desk.

Everyone has a point of view.
Some people call it style,
but what we're really talking about
is the guts of a photograph.
When you trust your point of view,
that's when you start taking pictures.

"Who said this?" Mrs. Pratt asks us,
tapping the marker against the board.

Before most kids finish reading the quote
I say, "Annie Leibovitz,"
my favorite photographer.

"Very good, Liz."

She tells the others
what I already know about Annie—
how she's most famous
for her portraits of celebrities,
how she takes risks with her art.

"Now it's your turn to take risks," Mrs. Pratt says.
"I want you each to create a self-portrait
that says something about you—
that shows the world your point of view."

Self-Portrait

At the end of class
I tell Mrs. Pratt I can't do this.
She says, "Yes, you can."

"I'll just throw a bag over my head
and take the shot.
Is that what you want?"

She matches my hard glare
with warm eyes.

When I read the syllabus
back in September
I couldn't wait to get to this assignment.

Now it's here and I don't want
to turn the lens toward me.

And He's Off

It's Thursday,
and when I come home
Mike's not here.

Uncle Nate told Mom and Dad
there was no need
to put everything on hold until the trial.

So Mike's gone back to Millbrook—
to his dorm,
his friends,
his life.

Friday

On my way to gym
I see kids
moving over
to the left side of the hall,
the right side
blocked
by three orange pylons
and Mr. Frick,
the janitor,
with his long, wide broom.
"Careful of the glass, kids,"
I hear him say.

I get closer
to where he stands
and nearly trip
over the gray rock
that shattered the display case
containing the homage
to my brother's feet.

Biological Germs

All week long the kids at school—
even the Nuisance
and Zero P—
look at me
and don't look at me
and stay as far away
from me
as possible.

Good-bye, Photogirl.

Hello,
Sister of a Rapist.

Changes

I come home to find my mother
in Mike's room
on the edge of his bed,
her hand smoothing over
the worn denim comforter.

I want to keep going but she looks so . . .
"Mom?"

She lifts her head and says,
"Hi, honey."
Her voice soothing, soft, sad.

"Mom, are you okay?"

"I'm okay, sweetie," she says,
looking down again to trace
the stitching of the spread with her finger.
"Everything will be okay."

She stands,
smooths out the spot she rose from,
and asks how school was.

"It was fine, Mom.
Just fine."

Painted Ponies

When the ferry docks
in Vineyard Haven
I take the island bus
to Oak Bluffs
and head up the street
to the Flying Horses Carousel
to get a shot
through a dirty window
of horses with no riders
brass ring out of reach.

Dead

Like an unprotected photograph,
some friendships fade.
People grow apart, lose touch,
want different things.
Dreams, woven together,
unravel.

But losing Kate
eats away at me
like a dirty old gull
picking at fresh prey.

Some days
I want to scream at that bird,
"I'm not dead, you stupid thing!
Leave me alone!"

Other days I lie there,
making no sound at all.
An offering.

Like Syrup on Sunday

Brian's on break next to me
in a booth near the kitchen.
We're sharing a heaping pile
of blueberry pancakes,
listening to his dad grilling
one of the new cooks.
"Is over easy too hard for you, Shandling?
Is your brain as scrambled as this order?"

A baby two booths down
wants no part of her high chair
and lets everyone on Cape Cod know.
A tray of silverware clatters to the floor
and a group of men laugh so hard
one shoots coffee out his nose.

I dip my last bit of breakfast into a
dark brown pool of sweetness
and let the sounds of normal
soak in.

Lather, Rinse

I head down the aisle in CVS and
when I reach out to grab a bottle of Pantene,
Kate's mom comes around the corner
swerving just quickly enough
to avoid collision.

The shampoo thuds to the floor
and rolls a foot away.
We both watch it go and come to a stop
before our eyes meet.

"Hello, Liz."
Stiff, formal.

"Hi, Carol."
Done.

She walks toward the prescription counter
as I hightail it to the exit,
the bottle of shampoo
still in the middle of aisle 9.

What does she think of me, this woman
who taught me how to make cookies from scratch?
Does she hate me? Blame me?
Does any part of her miss me?

Hallway Traffic

Amanda and Dee Dee both make
a high-speed attempt at smiling at me
and keep on going.

I know Kate can't stand
the sight of me.
I shouldn't be surprised
that they choose
to follow her lead.

I'm really starting
to hate them all.

But Most of All

I hate myself
because if I'd kept
my big mouth shut
there would have been no fight
no reason for me to go upstairs
and leave her
alone.

Mixed Emotions

I've seen these girls around school.
They're juniors, I think,
and they're too busy eating french fries
and talking about guys
to notice me in the booth behind them.

I'm waiting for Brian to go on break,
pretending to work on an English essay,
and listening to them as they spin out a list
of the hottest guys they know.

"Mike Grayson's cute," one of them says,
and I force myself not to lift my head.

"How can you say that?" the other girl asks.

"My brother used to run track with him
and I talked to him once when he hung out at my house."

"Really? Wow!"

"Yeah, *really*! There's no way he did that."

"You're probably right.
He doesn't look like a rapist to me."

I let out a sigh, then swallow hard.

Relief and disgust
are two emotions
not easily blended.

Undercover

"No one's really talking about it."
"*Of course* I'd tell you if they were."

I'm amazed at how smoothly these words
slide off my tongue,
a sled on a well-groomed hill.

The softening of lines on my mother's brow as I say them,
the way my father pats, then squeezes her hand,
is worth the shards of ice that slice
just beneath the layers of white.

Some Sailor

As I walk by the bridge
Dad waves and I wonder
how my father,
capable of navigating a trillion-ton boat
in all kinds of weather
and pulling her safely into port,
will steer his family
through this storm.

New Route

I imagine the ferry
making a sharp turn south,
her motors churning out
a wake of raging foam,
me
at the helm
heading for open water.

Sunday, November 16

Three a.m. beams blue
from the periwinkle clock
on the nightstand by my bed.

Four weekends since
our last and final
Saturday Night Slumber

Wide awake.
No slumbering here.

Portfolio Day

I should be glassy-eyed and cotton-headed
after a sleepless night,
but I'm pumped with adrenaline
as I enter the Hynes Convention Center.

This place is nuts.
So many kids, so many portfolios
so many lines, so little time.

I planned ahead,
got the layout of the hall online.

The woman from Parsons
has gray hair pulled back in such a tight bun
that for a moment I imagine
the skin on her forehead might tear off.
Her red eyeglasses hang
from a silver chain around her neck.

She just grinned at the girl in front of me
and said, "You've got your work cut out for you, dear."
I turn to watch the girl walk away
with her portfolio between her legs.

The woman tap, tap, taps her magnifying glass
against the table to get my attention.

"Do you have something to show me?"

The zipper sticks, and she lets out a sigh,
but then a "hmmm"
as she flips through the pages
of my portfolio.

"Not bad. You might want to
make this one a bit bigger,
and your matting could be a little neater,
but not bad at all."

My zipper sticks again
as I try to close the portfolio
and I hear her tapping.

But when I look up she gives me
a wink and a smile.

Warped Sense of Normal

For a few weeks things fall
into this strange rhythm.

I go to school
eat lunch with Brian
pretend that Kate
isn't sitting across the room.
I go to work
helping Randall
who at this rate will never
handle in-season crowds.
I go home
tell my parents
about my college applications
my high SATs.

And sometimes
if I try real hard
I can make myself believe
there's nothing left to say.

But . . .

Even if no one says it
the word rape
hums soft and constant
like water running
through the pipes in our walls.

Not Over the River or Through the Woods

We usually spend Thanksgiving
at Grandma Grayson's in Connecticut
but my father decided it was best
this year
for us to spend holidays at home.

Customer Assistance, Please

Mom has always been a talker,
making friends and conversation
wherever she goes.

We'd be in the supermarket
picking up pasta salad to bring to a picnic
and she'd start talking to the checkout lady—
when we were already running late—
complimenting the woman's ability
to scan items so quickly.

"See you soon!" Mom would chirp
when everything was bagged and in the cart.

"I hope so!" the lady would chirp back.

But Dad's the one at Bag & Buy now
shopping for our holiday meal
because, these days, Mom's words come
slowly and with effort
and she avoids public places,
keeps her eyes to the floor.

I want to run to Bag & Buy
and tell that checkout lady
to stop tallying up those turkeys

and call my mom *now*
because I have no idea
what to do to help her.

Giving Thanks

It's Thanksgiving
and I'm thankful
Mike's off skiing
with friends in Colorado.

Dinner and a Movie

Brian pulls into the driveway
and turns off the chariot's engine.
"That was fun," I say.

He kisses my neck
and everything fades away.
"And this is fun, too. . . ."
He kisses my lips. "And so is this. . . ."

He kisses me more
and I'm grateful
that he keeps going.

Despite the cold outside,
the windows and my entire body
steam up.

When he puts his hand
against my breast
sparks fly.

Wham! Wham!

We pull apart so fast
Brian hits his head
on the driver's-side window.

"Elizabeth Grayson! Get in the house now!"
My mother stands beside the car, her hand
shattering the barrier of careful words
she and I have been trying
so hard to build between us.

Brian Running

As Mom stomps toward the house
Brian rubs his face with his hands,
says he should go,
leans across me to open my door.

I've always admired his speed,
the way he zips around the track
leaving other guys
in the cloud of his dust.

But now I worry, someday soon,
he'll run away from me
and I'll be left
hunched over
alone and unable to catch up
choking
on all he's kicked behind.

Bzzzzz

I storm after Mom into the house.
"We weren't doing anything!
I was just kissing him good night!"

"It looked like more than that to me."

I fly up the stairs, hot on her heels.
"What were you doing? Spying on me?"

"I wasn't spying. I got worried
when you were both out there so long."

"Worried about what, Mom?
Worried that Brian would *rape* me?"

My words sting
and Mom flinches
before escaping to her room
leaving me in the hallway
still buzzing.

I Knew Nothing

After a fender bender last summer,
Mom screamed at Dad,
"You can pull a ferry into port,
but you can't avoid a mailbox
in your own stupid driveway!"

I thought that was family tension.

But I was wrong.
This.
This is family tension.

Final Portfolio Prep

Mrs. Pratt claps her hands.
"Time to get serious now, folks."

I stayed up late last night
rearranging things,
adding in the Vineyard shots,
taking out what no longer fit.

She leans over my shoulder,
her black wavy hair pulled back,
giving off a berry-infused scent.
"Liz, there's something about these pictures."

I'm waiting for her to go on,
to say how I've really dug deep this time,
how my photos are filled with intensity.
Instead, she puts her hands on my shoulders.
"It's like you're trying too hard."

I dig the nail of my middle finger
deep into the tip of my thumb.

"And you're forgetting simple things—
the exposure's off here,
no focal point here.
This one's good but would be better with a filter."

I wish she'd stop talking.
I get it already.
What's the point
of this damn portfolio
if I've lost my touch?

"Your original portfolio was really strong, Liz,
and portraits have always been your thing.
I don't see any portraits here."

I wish she would just
shut up.

"Maybe stop worrying about new photos
and go through some of your old ones."

I've lost my talent.
I can't do this anymore.
When I look through the lens now,
I no longer know who I see.

And I can't go back
to my old stuff.
It hurts too much.

Juggling Act

As tempting as it seems
I can't run off with the circus.
Because the only one that comes around here,
to the Barnstable County Fairgrounds,
doesn't come until July
and outside my window
Dad's stringing his hopes
along with white lights of Christmas.

Final Bell

The last bell rings and students cheer
as they leave Shoreview High for winter break.
I'm not cheering or leaving, though.
I'm heading to the art room.

"I'm glad you came," Mrs. Pratt says,
sitting at one of the long tables,
the photos I gave her yesterday
laid out before her.

When she first asked me to meet with her
I said no.
What was the point?

Then I decided the point
was to get into art school
and out of Shoreview.

"Tell me what you think are your strongest pieces."
I look at the photos of Kate.
I will not cry.
Instead, I shrug.

"Liz, I've tried not to pry,
because I thought that's what you wanted,
but I'm sure this has been hell for you."

My hands are clenched.
I will not cry.

"If you can't go through these now, I understand.
But there's great stuff here."

She holds up the photo of Kate
defying gravity with her soaring split.
My heart rips.
Tears flow.

Mrs. Pratt moves my photos
so they won't get wet
and pulls me into her arms.

And I don't worry if it's okay to cry—
I just do.

When the Tears Stop

I'm too wiped out to be mortified
but not too stupid to see
that Mrs. Pratt is right.

The original photos—
the portraits—
are the better ones.

I'll use these pictures to get into art school,
where I'll focus on something different
like landscape photography—
or still-life shots, where all aspects
are controlled by me.

As I'm getting ready to leave,
Mrs. Pratt pulls out a newer picture—
one I threw in to make sure
I had enough shots.

"I really love this one, too," she says.
"It's so interesting."

It's my self-portrait.

"It's not supposed to look like that," I say.
"I wanted the bag to cover my face,

but the timer went off before
I could pull it all the way down."

"Talk about how things
can be interpreted differently," she says,
turning the photo toward me.
"I thought you set the timer to catch yourself
taking the bag *off*."

Pit Stop

I'm so happy to be away from school,
sitting on the floor in Brian's room
opening my Christmas present.

It's a necklace, with a silver charm.
A palm tree.

"For Tahiti," he says,
and this in no way matches up
to the new pair of sneakers
wrapped in a box beside me.

I kiss him, long and slow,
until he pulls away.

"I have something to show you."
He gets up and goes over to his desk
grabs a thick manila envelope
and brings it to me.

The label, in the upper left corner, reads
UNIVERSITY OF MASSACHUSETTS AMHERST,
and I know what it means,
and I know that western Massachusetts
is eons away from the tropics.

He'd been hoping to get in,
early decision,
and he did.

I squeak out how happy I am
and bury my face as I hug him,
trying to hide my tears.

But I know he knows
when he squeezes me and says,
"It's not too far from wherever you'll be,
and just a pit stop on the way to Tahiti."

He wanted this.
He worked for it.
He deserves it.

But this pit stop isn't a rest area.
It's a crater, opening up
swallowing me whole.

Christmas Dinner

"Thanks for supporting me," Mike says,
when Mom finishes instructing Dad
on the proper way to carve a turkey.

"Don't be silly," Dad says,
lifting his eyes from the butchered bird.

Mom looks at Mike like he's handed her a present.
"Of course we support you."

Dad holds the platter out to me
and I stab a piece of meat with my fork,
choosing to give my family
the gift of silence.

New Year's Day

Brian's at a family brunch
that I didn't want to go to,
and I'm filling out college applications
because I've made a resolution
to get away.

I snort when I get to an essay choice
from the Museum School:
"What individual (artist or otherwise),
event, or personal experience
has had a profound effect on your art?"

I write about Annie Leibovitz
because she's a willful woman—
because she's
the easier choice.

Oh, Daddy

Dad comes in as I'm finishing the essay.
"How's the college stuff coming?"

I'm not sure he wants an answer,
maybe he's only asking so that
something
will fill the empty air that hangs between us.

I want to run into his arms
and give him a tight squeeze.
I want to tell him
everything.

I look up into his hazel eyes
and the laugh lines,
the ones he says he got
from smiling so hard
when his children were born,
now look like cracks in
hard, parched earth.

"It's coming along, Dad," I say,
pushing my chair back as I rise
onto the balls of my feet
and lean in to kiss
my father's weathered cheek.

Dipping

It's Sunday morning and I sit beside Mom
on the cream-colored couch in our living room.
I need to know some things
and this couch—
the only one in the house I'll sit on now—
is as comfortable a place as any
to search for answers.

While Mom pores over the obituaries,
a habit since Gramps died,
I reach for the front page of the *Cape Cod Times*.
The lead article, "The Polar Plunge,"
has a photo of folks smiling as they leap
into the icy surf at Bright Penny,
a yearly fund-raiser for cancer research.

"What if he's found guilty?" I ask,
stepping into unchartered seas.

"He won't be found guilty!" she says
with such force that I shift my gaze
and notice her hands clenching the paper,
her once-long nails chewed to nubs.

"But what if he is?"

She raises her eyes from the dead
and glares at me.
"Guilty? You think he's guilty?"

I jerk my feet out of the frigid water.
"I mean what if he's *found* guilty."

With this reworked sentence
her hands unclench
and she lays the paper on the table.

"He won't be," she says, as feeling begins
to return to my toes.

Done and Gone

Applications filled out.
Recommendations in sealed envelopes.
Slides of photos carefully arranged
in plastic slide-holder sheets.

I kiss each package in front
of the scruffy-faced man
who works at the Shoreview post office,
my lips chilled from February's frost.
He raises his eyebrows and says,
"Important stuff, huh?"

I nod and say, "Very,"
as he stamps the words
FRAGILE, HANDLE WITH CARE
onto my hopes for a future.

Some Celebration

It's early Friday evening
and Mom's taking me to dinner
to celebrate sending my portfolio off.

As we head toward The Big Surf,
she makes a quick turn.
"I just need to stop at Nate's to sign some papers."

So now, instead of pulling scallops
out of baked stuffed lobster,
I'm in Uncle Nate's office
sitting in this under-stuffed chair
covered with scratchy upholstery.

"Lizzie, I'd like to put you on the stand," he says.
I let out a short, high-pitched laugh
and turn to face Mom, who at any minute
will jump right in and tell him that's ridiculous.

But Mom's eyes keep shifting
from my face to her lap.
She says nothing.

"Is this why you brought me here?
You knew what he was going to ask me!"

My mother looks to Uncle Nate,
who stacks some folders,
opens a desk drawer,
puts the folders in.

"I just need you to establish a time line," he says.
"To say what time you left Kate and went upstairs."

He's still talking
but I can't make out the words
with the phrase *You left Kate*
echoing in my head.

Bird's-Eye View

The seagull is pecking
at a dead crab—
a Saturday afternoon snack.

"Can you put the camera down
for a minute and come over here?"

Brian's words distract me.
The bird flies off.

"Brian!" I jerk my head toward him,
the camera strap cutting into my neck.
"I missed the shot!"

He digs his hands deep
into the pockets of his jeans
and kicks at the sand,
"Well, I miss *you*."

Waves crash along the seawall
and a salty mist sprays his face.
I tell him there's nothing to miss,
that I'm right here—
that I came straight home from work
like he asked
to be with him.

"Yeah, you're here, all right.
Acting like everything's
picture-perfect."

I tell him that's not true,
that nothing's perfect,
as tears mix with sea spray
and I slump down onto the cold, damp sand.
"What am I supposed to do?
I'm a mess!"

"I don't think you're a mess," he says,
sitting down beside me,
taking hold of my hand,
his body a shield from the biting wind.

An Invitation

Brian tells me his cousin Cameron
is having a party tonight in Brewster,
that no one from school will be there.

I tell him I'm not up for a party,
that I just want to be with him.

"I want to be with you, too.
But there's nothing wrong
with hanging out with other people."

"Fine," I say. "Go hang out with other people, then."

He says he meant we should hang out
with other people
together.

I jump up—"You don't like being alone with me?
I'm too screwed up for you?"

"Damn it, Liz!" he says as he stands,
brushing sand off the back of his jeans.
"I don't think you're screwed up, but *you* do!"

I tell him he has no idea what I think.

"That's because you don't talk to me anymore," he says.
"Talk to me, Liz!"

I can't.
I want to but I can't.
And with each tick of silence
I see him sprinting away.
And if he leaves, what then?

I move two steps closer to him,
wrap my arms around his waist,
and bury my head in his coat.
"Okay, I'll go."

"What?" he asks,
putting his hands on my shoulders,
forcing me to look at him.

"I'll go to the party."

Maybe if I go,
he'll stay.

Jack Daniels in Brewster

The first sip sears
the lining of my throat.

I swallow hard
because I need to feel
something.

I swallow more
because I need to feel
nothing.

The Party Scene

Some guys are playing quarters
on the black granite island
in Cameron's kitchen.

I leave Brian there
and make my way to the family room
where music is playing,
couples getting close.

I'm warm and woozy
as I lean my body against a wall,
the vibrations of surround sound
massaging my back.

Cameron is sitting near me
in a maroon upholstered chair.
A girl with a purple stripe in her hair
is on his lap, facing him,
her knees bent over the chair's curved arms.

I'm close enough to hear her
as he slides his hands under her shirt.
She's telling him to stop.

He says, "Shhh,"
and I move toward them

in one long stride,
pulling her off him, the contents
of her blue plastic cup
splashing the chair, the wall,
her stark white blouse.

"Did you not hear her?" I scream.
"Because *I* did!"

She yells for me to let go of her arm,
Cameron says, "What the hell?"
and Brian is suddenly beside me,
leading me out the door.

Wake-Up Call

"Wake up, Liz, you're home," Brian says,
shaking my shoulder,
sending things spinning.

"What time is it?" I ask.

"Quarter to twelve."

I tell him it's early and he says,
"It's been a long night."

A sickly sweet taste
rises to my mouth.
I swallow it down and realize
the fuzzy dream I had earlier
was not a dream at all.

"Oh, Brian—"

He doesn't let me finish.
"Listen, Liz. I can't talk about this now, okay?"

He always turns off the engine
for a few minutes
when we get to my house.
But tonight the engine's still running.

"I'm really tired," he says.
"I just want to go home."

And I whisper in his ear, "I'm sorry,"
as he leans across me and opens my door.

He always waits until I'm inside
before driving away,
but the second my feet hit the lawn
the chariot disappears.

Watch Me

I run into the house
and head straight to my room,
but not before Mom comes out of the bathroom
and catches a glimpse of me
bawling my eyes out.

She's standing in my doorway now
wringing her hands.
A modern-day Lady Macbeth.

"I'm your mother!" she's wailing.
"Please tell me what's wrong!"

I shake my head and slam the door.

Mike's future
may be spent behind bars but
right now
everything's clanging shut
in a home on Fairview Terrace.

Red Means Go

I'm sitting on the chariot's hood
when Brian gets off work.
He sees I'm here,
his shoulders slump,
but he holds the door open
for me to get in.

"You okay?" he asks
as we leave the parking lot.

"I'm so sorry, Brian.
I'm *really* sorry.
Are we okay?"

He says the worst thing.
He says he's not sure.

"I told you I didn't want to go to the party!"

"Yeah, that's right," he says. "You told me."

He grips the steering wheel,
keeps his eyes on the road.

"Brian!"
I don't even try to stop the tears from coming.

He leans over and opens the glove box,
hands me a pack of tissues.
"I just don't know what to do anymore, Liz."

I ask him what that's supposed to mean
and he says he can't make me happy.
But that's so silly because he *can*, he *does*.
"I *am* happy. I'm happy with *you*!"

"Well, I'm not happy, Liz."

And with those words
a silence drops
like a curtain at the end of a play.

I ask him if he's breaking up with me
and he says he doesn't know what he's doing anymore,
that right now he's just taking me home.
"Let me save you the trouble," I say,
reaching for the door handle.
"Pull over."

He shakes his head,
tells me he's not leaving me
in the middle of the road.

"Yes, you are," I tell him.
And at the next red light
I'm gone.

What Do I Know?

It's amazing how you think
you know someone so well,
then one day you come to see
that you really don't know
that person at all.

And you wonder
what that says
about you.

Off the Hook

When I get home
I can't escape to my room
because Mom's sitting on my bed.
Without even looking at me she says,
"We talked to Uncle Nate—"

"I don't care!
I don't care about Uncle Nate
or the trial
or anything!"

Now, she looks.
"Lizzie, what's wrong?"
She moves toward me
but I back away.

"Brian and I just broke up.
Not that *you* care!"
I try not to cry
but it doesn't work.

"Oh, honey, I'm so sorry," she says.
"Of course I care."

"No, you don't!"

She grabs a tissue from my nightstand
and hands it to me.
"Is that what you think?" she asks.

How could I *not*?
There's no way the hell of my life
could match up in her eyes
to what my brother's going through.

"I'm sorry, Liz," she says,
raising her arms in the air.
"I'm doing the best I can!"

I tell her, "I know.
But it's not enough."

She's quiet for a minute
and I feel sad for her, sad for us.
I wait for her to put her arms around me—
to tell me that she really wants to hear about Brian—
when the phone rings.

"That's probably Nate, he said he'd call me right . . ."
I tell her she'd better answer it then,
and she hesitates a second
before heading to the kitchen
to take the call.

Framing

The Nuisance hangs my self-portrait,
the one with the bag half-on
or half-off,
on the wall in the art room.

Mrs. Pratt points to it,
telling us that she loves
the way it makes her think
about the subject, about the taker.

"Me too," says The Brenda Show.

I used to love this part of class,
where Mrs. Pratt focuses
on a particular aspect of a shot
and everyone shares their thoughts.

But this time it's all about me,
and I no longer like the spotlight.
"I told you it wasn't supposed to look like that.
It doesn't tell the whole story."

"I know, Liz," she says,
and the Hoopster adds,
"You can't sum up a whole life in a 5x7."

Reality Hits

There were moments,
up until this one,
when I could forget about the trial.
I was taking photos,
working extra shifts,
watching The Brenda Show
when I had some downtime.

But now it's April
and here he is,
Nike sneakers on the landing,
orange toothbrush by the sink,
Cap'n Crunch back
on the pantry shelf.

And I'm pissed off
watching him,
feet up on the coffee table,
remote in hand,
lounging
on *that* couch.
"How can you sit there?"

"What?"
He flips the channel.

"How can you so casually
sit *there*?"

He turns to look at me.
"Would you like it better
if I were sitting in jail?"

I take too long to answer
because what I'd like
is for none of this to have happened.

"Yeah. That's what I thought," he says,
turning back to watch TV.

Almost Over

On Friday morning, as we drive
to the Barnstable County Courthouse,
Mom turns to Dad and says, "We'll get past this."

She says *this* as if it's a marker in the road like:
Once we get over the Bourne Bridge we can stop to pee.

But instead of being sturdy,
made of steel,
this feels like something
too rickety to cross.

Bearing Witness

"That's not right!" I say,
when Uncle Nate tells me I'm sequestered—
that I can't be in the courtroom
during any testimony but my own.

"I'm sorry, but it's the law."

This doesn't fly with Mom.
"The jury should see that we all support Mike!"
That's her need, not mine.

I do want to be there
but for different reasons.

Even though
nothing I say can help Kate,
and what I do say
might make things worse,
I want to be
in that courtroom
to make up for not being
downstairs.

Sequestered

I do my time in the witness room
watching made-for-TV movies,
trying to keep my mind off the show
taking place down the hall—
the one without a scripted ending.

But I can't help wondering
if she's on the stand yet,
if Uncle Nate is making her feel
like she's the one on trial.

At around one p.m.
Mom, Dad, Uncle Nate, and Mike come in.
Dad says to me, "The first part is over.
They presented their case.
After lunch, it's our turn."

"What did Kate say?
Is she okay?"

My brother crosses the room
like he's in a meet.
"What do you mean, is she okay?
I could go to jail because of her!"

It's true. He could go to jail.
But will he?
And if he does,
whose fault would that be?

All Eyes on Me

It's odd to be called as a "witness"
when I didn't witness
a damn thing.

Taking the Stand

Kate's not allowed in here—
she's sequestered, too—
but as I move up the aisle
I see Amanda and Dee Dee
seated behind Kate's parents.

Dee Dee gives me a warm look
and I can't tell if it's pity or compassion
and I'm not sure it matters anymore.

I sweep my eyes around the room
when I reach my spot on the stand.
Brian's not here and I know there's no reason
for me to expect he would be.

Still, I stare at the courtroom doors
hoping he'll burst through them
like tape at the finish line,
but he's finished with me.

My family is here.
Mike, his hand on his temple,
Mom and Dad behind him,
staring at me, willing love
or their idea of the right words
my way.

To Tell the Truth

My throat is dry
my body is shaking
I keep thinking I'll say
the wrong thing.

Uncle Nate sticks
to the questions we went over,
and I'm sure, to the jury,
they seem pretty straightforward,
but answering them on the stand
feels a hell of a lot different
than it did in his office.

When he gets to the question
about why I went upstairs,
I say we had a fight.

He asks what we fought about
and I tell him,
"I thought her boyfriend was boring,
I told her she was staying with him and giving up dance
because she was afraid to take risks."

What made me think getting that off my chest
in this room, of all places,
would make me feel better?

"It would be taking a risk
for her to have sex with your brother, wouldn't it?"

"Yes, but . . ."

"Thank you, Miss Grayson.
No further questions, Your Honor."

Yes and Yes and Yes and . . .

"How long have you known Ms. Morgan?"
"About ten years."

"And you were best friends for most of that time?"
"Proud to be her friend?"
"Trusted her?"
"Shared personal secrets?"
"Called her your 'forever-best' friend, didn't you?"
"You are aware that Ms. Morgan has claimed she was raped?"
"You understand rape is a serious charge?"
"That one convicted of rape might lose not only his reputation but also his freedom?"
"And you understand that, even though it's not fair, being raped might damage the victim's own reputation?"
"And yet Ms. Morgan has come forth to say that she was raped by the defendant, right?"
"Would it be fair to say that someone who would make up such a story would be dishonest and dishonorable?"
"And for all the years you've known Ms. Morgan, have you known her—your 'forever-best'— to be a dishonest and dishonorable person?"

"Objection!" Uncle Nate calls out, and the defense attorney withdraws the question.

"Now, Ms. Morgan has reported that she was raped in her

best friend's house, right?"
"And you're that best friend?"
"She has reported that this horrible crime occurred while her best friend was sleeping upstairs, right?"
"That was you sleeping?"
"And she has reported that the rapist was her best friend's brother, correct?"
"That was your brother?"
"Now I would expect that someone who had a houseguest raped in her own house might feel shame. Would you agree?"
"And that shame might be double in intensity if that houseguest were a friend, and perhaps double again in intensity if that friend were a best friend. Would you agree?"
"Now, Ms. Grayson, you've known Ms. Morgan for years. Your friend, trusted confidante, your 'forever-best.' Do you think she is the sort of sick person who would lie to make you feel that sort of shame?"

Uncle Nate jumps to his feet. "Objection! Argumentative."

The judge says, "Sustained."

"Now, you love your brother, right?"
"And, while friends are friends, blood runs deep?"
"Would you do anything for your brother?"

"I wouldn't lie for him about something like this."

Fast and Furious

These questions fire at me
like the clicks of camera
set on continuous mode.

But memories
of a brother, a best friend,
the worst night of our lives,
are impossible to fit
into the frame of yes-no responses
I'm expected to give.

So they swell up inside me.

Until there are no more questions
until there is no more space
until I leave the courtroom
in a flood of tears.

Adjourned

At the end of the day
I scan the hall for Kate
but I don't see her.

Closing arguments
are Monday morning.
We should have a verdict
by Monday afternoon.

"I think things went well," Uncle Nate says,
and congratulates Mike
for keeping cool on the stand,
congratulates me, too.

As we leave the courthouse
I put my hand to my mouth
to keep from throwing up
all over Uncle Nate's
shiny black shoes.

Natural Light

I'm looking to do anything
to keep my mind busy this weekend.

I haven't taken a portrait in a long time,
but Mrs. Pratt wants one taken in natural light,
and the sun glistens off the water
as I come down the ferry ramp.

I see an old man at the water's edge
in a drab woolen coat.
He's tossing bits of bread into the sea.

I lift my camera and zoom in,
waiting for the world to go silent.
As I hold the camera steady,
I'm moved by his desire to feed the fish.

Suddenly, gulls swoop down
snatching fish and bread
with sharp, angry beaks.
More join in—swooping,
snatching, screeching.

Is the old man here
to feed the fish,
or set a trap for them?

The ferry horn blows
and the man walks away.
His bag of bread empty,
my camera full of unused film.

Viewfinder

As the man disappears from view,
I think of the portraits I've taken—
the ones Mrs. Pratt calls
my "best work."

Who's to say the woman
mowing her lawn
is longing to be somewhere else?

Maybe the boy's joyful look
has nothing to do
with old wooden horses.

I control the exposure
with my f-stop
and my light meter
and my shutter speed.

I wait for the moment
when things are as I want them to be.

Then I click and think
that says it all.

But it says nothing.

And instead of “Preparing My Shot,”
all I can think of now is:
“Photography Means Shit.”

Aftershock

I've lost
my best friend
my boyfriend
and my PMS mood.

All I have left
are my parents
on a live wire,
my brother
close to the third rail,
and my need
to connect to something.

Flash

I grab the shoulder strap of my camera,
rush toward the beach,
and swing the stupid useless thing
again and again
against a rough wooden pylon.

"Hey! Hey there! No, Lizzie! No!"

My father—
my so-slow-lately, so-careful father—
runs like a madman down the ramp,
grabs from my trembling hands
what's left of my once favorite thing.

"He did it, Daddy. I think he did it."

My heart stops.
I feel it seize and stop.
I didn't mean to say those words.
What have I just done?
WhathaveIjustdone???

My father turns the camera over
in his big, soft hands,
takes in the shattered lens,
the cracked shutter.

"I'm sorry, Daddy. I'm so sorry!"
I'm crying so hard my head throbs.

He lays the camera on the ground
and pulls me into his arms.
"You, Lizzie, have nothing to be sorry for."

"Yes, I do, Daddy!
I've screwed up everything!"

"So you're not perfect, Lizzie.
No one is.
But you're not
not perfect
because of Mike."

I look up and see Randall
coming toward us.
He takes a few steps. Stops.
Takes a few more.
"Um, Liz? Is everything all right?"

"She's okay," my father tells him,
and I'm not sure I am,
but the words he said to me wrap
like an Ace bandage
around my heart.

Images

I'm in the courtroom
seated with my parents
behind my brother's table
as the judge instructs the jury.

Every moment
of the past six months
has led to this.

The lawyers have finished closing statements
(Kate's a slut. Mike's evil.),
both creating images to show someone
the way they want them to be seen.

I used to be so confident
about who people were, who I was—
that woman's a gossip, that guy's a prick,
I'm a girl with a camera and something to say.

But, while listening to the lawyers plead their case, I realized
I no longer see things
in crisp black-and-white contrasts—
some things come in shades of gray,
hues that give pause and make me wonder,
make me want to know more.

And I think about what Javier said,
how you can't sum up a whole life in a 5x7.
And now I get it.

But I wonder if maybe there's still room
for catching magic in a moment
where a woman seems wistful,
or a boy, excited.

Where a girl,
as she dances,
looks lighter than air.

Verdict

The forewoman stands,
looks down at the paper,
looks up at the judge,
and says in a voice that does not waver,

"We the jury
find the defendant,
Michael James Grayson,
not guilty."

Mom and Dad jump up, crying, and lean
over the banister, clutching my brother,
who lets out an audible sigh of relief.

Mom's saying, "Yes! Yes!"
like she's just won
a million dollars on a game show.

But I feel like a buzzer should sound
instead of a bell.
I think the jury got it wrong.
And this is the tricky part:
I'm glad that they did.

Better or Worse?

I don't think he meant it
but I think he did it.
Was this justice?
I don't think so.

But the thought
of my brother
rotting away in a cell
is almost as hard to take
as the thought of my mother
walking around like a zombie—
not dead, but not alive—
of my father trailing behind her
picking up parts as they fall.

The Other Side

Kate's father makes a guttural sound,
her mother yells, "No!"
and they both reach for their daughter,
who is rocking back and forth,
eyes closed.

I wince,
let out a silent sigh,
a silent *I'm so sorry*,
then close my eyes, too,
hug her in my mind,
and pray she can feel it.

Shades of Memory

It's Tuesday morning, one day down,
and I'm back in Mrs. Pratt's room
cleaning up my space before class ends.
Javier comes over and sits down beside me.

"Hi, Liz."

"Hi, Javier."

He's cracking his knuckles,
something he always does
while sitting on the bench
before a big game.

"So, I was thinking . . . ," he says,
and I wonder if he's thinking
what an annoying habit that is.

But he seems so nervous
so I just say, "What?"

He covers one hand with the other
and asks me if I'll be his date
for the prom.

His question sends a tingle through my body,
something I haven't felt in a long time.
A tingle, I now know,
I'm capable of feeling again.

But all I can see
are pages of a magazine
with photos of two dresses,
in shades of pale yellow and sea-foam green,
and two girls cutting those pages out,
tacking them to a bulletin board
in a room filled with dance trophies.

"I'm sorry, Javier. I just can't."

And I leave the room before the bell rings,
before the cracking starts again,
before he can ask me why.

Picture This

It's been a week since the trial
and Mom's sitting at the kitchen table,
next to me, our chairs pushed close,
shoulder touching shoulder,
looking through my portfolio.

It's a quiet moment
in sharp contrast to twenty minutes ago
when I opened my acceptance letter
from Parsons School of Design.

She's oohing and aahing
over photos old and new
and I'm glad for the return
of her singsong sounds.

"I've missed looking at your work," she says,
and I'm happy because she voiced
the words I hoped to hear.
And because I believe her.

She reaches for a picture
taken from the rear of her and Dad
as they sat together last spring
on the wrought-iron bench
in our garden out back.

"I remember that day," she tells me.
"The irises were coming up."
A real and true smile graces her lips.
"I didn't know, sneaky girl,
you were hiding out behind us."

I tell her I remember, too.
And that I loved the way she and Dad
sat silent, holding hands,
leaning into one another,
watching flowers bloom.

"I'm surprised we didn't hear you."
She puts the picture down,
reaches for another.

"That's because I was PMSing," I say.

And it doesn't hurt
this time
to say it.

Minor and Major

It's the middle of first period
and the hallway is empty
as I bring a note from Mrs. Pratt
to the principal's office.

I stop at the wall near the cafeteria,
papered with college-acceptance letters.
I find my letter there.

Then I search until I find hers.
Kate's going to Cornell.

"Impressive, huh?"

I flinch, because I didn't hear Amanda coming.
For a girl who talks nonstop,
she's surprisingly quiet on her feet.

"Yeah, it is. I'm happy for her."

"Congrats on Parsons, by the way. I'm going to BU."

Even though we still have classes together,
Amanda and I haven't talked this much in ages.

"You holding up okay?" she asks,
gently squeezing my arm.
Her hand is warm.

"I'm holding up."

"Kate's holding up, too. She's decided to minor in dance."

Hearing this makes me want to hug Amanda,
because Kate minoring in dance
is a major-good thing.
But I don't hug her because it still stings
not hearing Kate's news from Kate.

Before I can say "That's great,"
Amanda's mouth moves again.
"Anyway, I gotta go. I was supposed to be making a quick trip to the bathroom and then I saw you and if I don't hurry up my bladder will burst and it won't be pretty."

My head throbs listening to her,
but my heart feels lighter.

Baby Steps

I'm at my desk
looking over the stuff from Parsons
when the phone rings.
My mother calls to me from the kitchen,
"Lizzie! Pick up. It's Mike."

He's been back at school for two weeks now,
we haven't talked since the trial,
and I reread a sentence about dorm life four times
before picking up the phone.

"Hey," I say,
in a bad attempt to sound casual.

"Hey," he says back,
and there's too long a pause until he adds,
"Congrats on getting in."

I tell him "Thanks,"
trying to push from my brain
an image of him running through the door,
picking me up from behind, spinning me around
in a fit of brotherly pride.

There's another pause before he says,
"Well, I gotta get going."

I say, "Okay, bye."
The line goes dead.

And I'm left feeling
things I can't explain
because I'm not sure
how to be his sister anymore.

I don't know how to forgive him,
especially since he doesn't think
he did anything wrong.

And I'm not sure he forgives me
for not believing him.

Maybe someday we'll sit
across from one another
in some therapist's office
and try to find a way to be okay.
But I'm not willing to do that yet,
and neither is he.

At least that's one thing
we can agree on.

Pomp and Circumstance

As I walk to the podium,
I hear the familiar sound
of my father's "Wahoo!"
even though people were asked
to hold their applause
until the last diploma is given.

I get back to my seat,
between Jacob Gorman and Stephanie Griggs,
four years of my life on my lap
in an embossed, padded folder.

When they call out "Brian Joseph Kent,"
he holds his diploma high over his head
then gives me that smile and a thumbs-up
as he passes my row.

I nod and smile back,
my heart warming a bit as my hand
touches the spot, just below the base of my neck,
where our palm tree rests.

"Katherine Cecily Morgan"

Who will be her maid of honor?
Which friend will hold her baby first?
Who will sit beside her
on a summer porch swing,
when hairs gray and memories start to fade,
and remind her that she was once
The Mistress of Modern Dance,
Photogirl's forever-best?

Not me.
It won't be me.

Memorial Day

I'm sitting on the stone jetty at Bright Penny
holding my brand-new Canon,
a graduation gift from Mom and Dad.

It's warmer than usual for this time of year
and the first hints of summer,
in bathing suits and stark white skin,
make their way onto the beach.

I'm panning the shoreline,
not really looking for a great shot,
just enjoying the feel of this new,
familiar object in my hands.

Through the lens someone catches my eye
and I worry, once I know I've been spotted,
that she'll think I was aiming at her.

Kate holds a book in her right hand;
a light green towel hangs around her shoulders.

She doesn't come over,
doesn't put her towel down,
but clutches it to her chest with her free hand,
like she's protecting herself from the wind
or maybe from me.

I want to tell her I'm sorry,
sorry she got hurt,
sorry for so many things.

I want to remind her that she once said,
"Everything lives on through history."
And let her know that I think
that means the good stuff, too.

But she won't be able to hear me.
She's too far away.

So I stand
and walk
toward her.

This Girl

She doesn't run off,
though her eyes tell me
she wonders if she should.

"Hi," I say, once I reach her,
gripping on to my camera like a lifeboat.

Then, in a rush of words that tumble like waves,
I tell her I'm sorry about the trial,
sorry that she had to go through that.

She looks past me toward the water,
as if she's searching for something.
"I'm sorry he wasn't convicted,
but I'm not sorry I testified."

She turns her eyes from the surf
to look straight into mine.
"As scary as it was,
I said what I needed to say."

And she did.

This girl,
who I never thought would take a risk,
has done exactly that.

Not far from where we stand,
a mother in a straw hat pulls
a red plastic shovel from her beach bag
and gives it to her toddler.

A horn blows
as a ferry carries its heavy load
across the sound.

"Bye, Liz," Kate says.
She releases her grip on the towel
and turns to go.

The toddler giggles, a gull cries,
water laps against the stones of the jetty.
Kate's footprints form a path behind her.
She doesn't look back.

And I raise my camera as she walks,
bathed in morning light,
across the sand we grew up on.
As sound fades away, I remember
the words of Annie Leibovitz:
When you trust your point of view,
that's when you start taking pictures.

This girl
is starting now.

The Rape, Abuse, and Incest National Network (RAINN) is the nation's largest anti-sexual-assault organization. RAINN operates the National Sexual Assault Hotline at 1-800-656-HOPE (4673). The National Sexual Assault Online Hotline, as well as many helpful resources, can be found on their website at rainn.org.

acknowledgments

There are many people to whom I am indebted for their support and sage advice during the writing of this novel:

To my mother, my brother, my sister, and all of my extended family, for always believing in me.

To Julio Thompson, for his legal expertise.

To Judy Cronin, chair of the Unified Arts Department at Dartmouth High School, and Christine McFee, teacher extraordinaire, for allowing me to shadow the darkroom photography class over the course of a school year. And to the students in that class who put up with my learning curve and my endless questions.

To the world's most fantabulous writers group: Carolyn DeCristofano, Deanna Garland, Leslie Guccione, Valerie Kerzner, Brian Lies, Wiesy MacMillan, Barbara O'Connor, Delia Weikert, and Mary Wisbach.

To Cindy Lord, Nancy Werlin, and Diane M. Davis, for much-needed early encouragement.

To Linda Urban, for being my "Go To" girl.

To Alma Fullerton, for all the late-night plotting (and plodding!) sessions.

To Tracie Vaughn Zimmer, my poetic muse, for your careful ear and your gentle soul.

To Sarah Aronson, for your friendship, for multiple reads, and most especially for suggesting I try writing a few scenes in poetry to see where that might lead.

To Stacy DeKeyser and Audrey Vernick, beautiful writers and equally beautiful friends, for all the thoughtful critiquing, hand-holding, and necessary butt-kicking and for always, always being there.

To Joy Peskin, for first encouraging me to try my hand at writing a novel and for your long-standing support and belief both in my writing and in me. This novel would not exist without you. Go, Daled!

To Tracey and Josh Adams, the "dynamic duo" of Adams Literary, for taking me under your wings and helping me soar. I am so lucky to have you both in my corner!

To Ellice Lee, rock-star art director, for designing a cover that so perfectly zooms in to the heart of this story. And to the Comma Queens of Copyediting, and the rest of the amazing Random House crew, for the wonderful work you do.

To Shana Corey, for totally "getting" this book from the get-go. Your keen eye and gently probing questions have taught me so much about how to push a story to the next level. And your enthusiasm and warm, bubbly personality make you a dream editor. A million thanks!

And lastly, to Jake and Abby, with all my love, for being wonderful children and for your willingness to eat too much take-out food while I wrote this book. And to Jon, for being the best friend and husband I could ever have hoped for. I love you.